FOREVER STARTS TONIGHT

Bachelors & Bridesmaids #6

BARBARA FREETHY

HYDE STREET PRESS
Published by Hyde Street Press
**1325 Howard Avenue, #321, Burlingame, California
94010**

© Copyright 2017 by Hyde Street Press

Forever Starts Tonight is a work of fiction. All incidents, dialogue and all characters are products of the author's imagination and are not to be construed as real. Any resemblance to persons living or dead is entirely coincidental.

All rights reserved. In accordance with the U.S. Copyright Act of 1976, the scanning, uploading, and electronic sharing of any part of this book without the permission of the publisher is unlawful piracy and theft of the author's intellectual property. No part of this book may be used or reproduced in any manner whatsoever without written permission except in the case of brief quotations embodied in critical articles and reviews.

Printed in the United States of America

Cover design by Damonza.com

ISBN: 978-1-944417-26-0

PRAISE FOR THE NOVELS OF
#1 NEW YORK TIMES BESTSELLING AUTHOR
BARBARA FREETHY

"In the tradition of LaVyrle Spencer, gifted author Barbara Freethy creates an irresistible tale of family secrets, riveting adventure and heart- touching romance."
-- *NYT Bestselling Author **Susan Wiggs** on Summer Secrets*

"This book has it all: heart, community, and characters who will remain with you long after the book has ended. A wonderful story."
-- *NYT Bestselling Author **Debbie Macomber** on Suddenly One Summer*

"Freethy has a gift for creating complex characters."
-- ***Library Journal***

"Barbara Freethy is a master storyteller with a gift for spinning tales about ordinary people in extraordinary situations and drawing readers into their lives."
-- ***Romance Reviews Today***

"Freethy's skillful plotting and gift for creating sympathetic characters will ensure that few dry eyes will be left at the end of the story."
-- ***Publishers Weekly** on The Way Back Home*

"Freethy skillfully keeps the reader on the hook, and her tantalizing and believable tale has it all– romance, adventure, and mystery."
-- ***Booklist** on Summer Secrets*

"Freethy's story-telling ability is top-notch."
-- ***Romantic Times** on Don't Say A Word*

"Powerful, absorbing...sheer hold-your-breath suspense."
-- *NYT Bestselling Author* **Karen Robards**
on *Don't Say A Word*

"A page-turner that engages your mind while it tugs at your heartstrings...Don't Say A Word has made me a Barbara Freethy fan for life!"
-- *NYT Bestselling Author* **Diane Chamberlain**
on *Don't Say a Word*

"I love *The Callaways*! Heartwarming romance, intriguing suspense and sexy alpha heroes. What more could you want?"
-- *NYT Bestselling Author* **Bella Andre**

"Once I start reading a Callaway novel, I can't put it down. Fast-paced action, a poignant love story and a tantalizing mystery in every book!"
-- *USA Today Bestselling Author* **Christie Ridgway**

"Barbara manages to weave a perfect romance filled with laughter, love, a lot of heat, and just the right amount of suspense. I highly recommend *SO THIS IS LOVE* to anyone looking for a sexy romance with characters you will love!"
-- **Harlequin Junkie**

"I adore *The Callaways*, a family we'd all love to have. Each new book is a deft combination of emotion, suspense and family dynamics. A remarkable, compelling series!"
-- *USA Today Bestselling Author* **Barbara O'Neal**

"*BETWEEN NOW AND FOREVER* is a beautifully written story. Fans of Barbara's Angel's Bay series will be happy to know the search leads them to Angel's Bay where we get to check in with some old friends."
-- ***The Book Momster Blog***

Also By Barbara Freethy

Bachelors & Bridesmaids
Kiss Me Forever (#1)
Steal My Heart (#2)
All Your Loving (#3)
Before I Do (#4)
Falling Into You (#5)
Forever Starts Tonight (#6)
Dreaming of You (#7), *Coming Soon!*

The Callaway Series
On A Night Like This (#1)
So This Is Love (#2)
Falling For A Stranger (#3)
Between Now and Forever (#4)
Nobody But You (Callaway Wedding Novella)
All A Heart Needs (#5)
That Summer Night (#6)
When Shadows Fall (#7)
Somewhere Only We Know (#8)
If I Didn't Know Better (#9)
Tender Is The Night (#10)
Take Me Home (A Callaway Novella)
Closer To You (#11)
Once You're Mine (#12) *Coming Soon!*

Lightning Strikes Trilogy
Beautiful Storm (#1)
Lightning Lingers (#2)
Summer Rain (#3)

Standalone Novels
Almost Home
All She Ever Wanted
Ask Mariah
Daniel's Gift
Don't Say A Word
Golden Lies
Just The Way You Are
Love Will Find A Way
One True Love
Ryan's Return
Some Kind of Wonderful
Summer Secrets
The Sweetest Thing

One

"Come back here, you coward." Jessica Blake scrambled through the house in hot pursuit, her high heels slipping and sliding on the newly waxed hardwood floors. By the time she reached the kitchen, the only evidence of escape was a swinging screen door and a guilty look on her seven-year-old son's face. She skidded to a stop. "Brandon, you didn't."

"He didn't mean it, Mom. You scared him."

She shook her head at the pointed accusation. "He has my wallet. Where did he go?"

"I don't know."

"Brandon..."

"In the backyard." Brandon followed her through the kitchen door. "You're not going to make him go away, are you? He was just teasing you."

"Teasing?" she echoed. No, taking her wallet went beyond teasing. It was definitely malicious behavior, probably brought on by their new surroundings. None of them had quite adjusted to their move from Southern to Northern California two months earlier. New city, new house, new school, new job…which was also why she wasn't in the mood to play games.

With a sigh, she strode over to the far end of the yard and planted her fists on her waist. "Okay, Wiley. I want my wallet. Now."

The only retort was an excited bark. Jessica squatted down and peered into the doghouse. "I've got some juicy meat bones for you, just the kind you like."

Brandon peered over her shoulder. "He's not going to believe you, Mom. You never give him bones."

She threw him a disgusted look. "Do you have any better ideas?"

"Maybe if you talk to him real nice."

"Why don't you talk to him?"

"Okay." Brandon clicked his fingers together enticingly. "Come on, boy. Let's go to school."

Wiley barked in response and bolted out of the doghouse pushing Jessica over on her rear end, covering the back of her navy-blue skirt in dirt. Wiley paused for a split second, sensing another disaster, and then tore off in a different direction as Jessica got up and sent him a scathing look.

"That's great. Only he didn't bring out my wallet."

"Do you want me to get it?" Brandon asked.

Jessica looked at his troubled face and shook her head. From here on out, she was fighting her own battles, even if this one was only between her and the dog. "I'll do it. Get your backpack. We're already late for school. I never should have brought this doghouse with us. It cost a fortune to ship it up here."

"But Daddy made it for me and Wiley."

Jessica's lips tightened at the mention of her ex-husband. Kevin Blake would not have been caught dead pounding nails into boards. And he'd only sent the doghouse because every few years he remembered he had a son, and tried to make up for his absence with some big gesture that usually only complicated her life. But she wasn't going to take away Brandon's love for his father with her own sour thoughts.

"Get your things, Brandon. We'll talk about it later."

With a quick look down at her skirt, Jessica shook her head in disgust. Getting down on all fours, she poked her head into the doghouse and squinted her eyes in the dark light. She reached her hand into the interior and groped around for her wallet. She came up with nothing.

Pushing herself farther into the doghouse until both her shoulders were inside the door, she stretched out her arm, her fingers reaching the tip of the leather billfold, but it wasn't quite enough. The wood around the door to the doghouse jabbed into her side, but she took in a deep breath and pushed forward. Her hand came around the wallet and she grabbed it triumphantly, but when she tried to back out, nothing gave. She pushed again, but the wood squeezed her body even tighter. A touch of panic went off in her mind as the darkness enveloped her, and it suddenly didn't seem that easy to breathe.

"Brandon," she yelled. "Help me get out of here."

Her son didn't answer, and she screamed louder, thinking he was probably in the house. "Brandon," she yelled again. "I need help."

"What's the matter?" Brandon asked breathlessly. "Did you find the wallet?"

"Yes, I found the wallet. Now I'm stuck. I need

you to pull on my legs. Can you do that for me, please?"

"Okay," he said, eager to help.

He grabbed her legs as she tried to push backward, but the wood refused to give. He gamely tried again, but it was no use. "I can't do it, Mommy. How did you get stuck?"

"I don't know." She rested her head on her hands as she considered the problem. Their next-door neighbor was a cranky old man, who didn't like to answer his door. The couple on the other side always left early for work, and she didn't want to send her seven-year-old across the street by himself.

"It's okay, Mom. I know what to do," Brandon said. "They told us in school yesterday."

She heard his feet scramble around the doghouse. A sudden uneasiness hit her as his words sank in.

"Wait a minute. Where are you going?" she yelled.

No answer.

"Brandon, go next door and get Mr. Gustavson."

No answer.

She drew in a deep breath, trying to suck in her body as much as possible. Using her palms for leverage, she pushed back against the wood as hard as she could. Her only reward was a stinging graze in her midriff where her blouse parted from her skirt. Slivers of wood stuck into her skin, and she bit back a cry of pain.

This was just what she needed. Two months in Half Moon Bay, and so far she'd dealt with the burst of a water pipe, lost her new couch in the move when it accidentally fell off the truck, and had discovered that every problem child in her new school had been put into her classroom.

Now this! What else could possibly go wrong?

Then she heard the sirens.

Loud and shrill, they blared through the still air of the suburban neighborhood, and for a split second she tried to tell herself there was a fire somewhere down the street. But the noise got louder until it finally stopped, followed by a rush of feet that made the ground tremble beneath her palms.

She heard a voice, low and husky and very masculine, with just enough laughter in the tone to make her blood boil.

"Mother stuck in a doghouse, just like the dispatcher said. This must be our day, Bill."

"Who's there?" Jessica called.

"Your local fire department," a man said.

"Can you get me out of here?"

"I sure hope so," he said with a chuckle deep in his throat. "Is that your mom in there, son?"

"Yes, and she's stuck," Brandon said importantly. "I called 911, just like they said in school."

Jessica groaned as she heard their conversation. She tried to wiggle out, but there was no escaping, and her cheeks began to burn as she thought of the picture she must be making with her rear end hanging out of the doghouse and her skirt hitched up around her thighs. A flush of heat swept through her body and for a second, she wished she could stay in the doghouse forever, but the touch of a hand on her thigh brought her quickly back to reality.

"What are you doing?" she demanded.

"Just checking things out," he said. "Mind if I ask why you're in there?"

"I was looking for my wallet."

"In the doghouse?"

"Wiley brought it in here."

"Who's Wiley?"

"Our dog," Brandon interrupted. "Can you get her out?"

"Is the dog in there too?"

"No, he's not," Jessica retorted. "The coward took off when he saw me coming."

"He was scared," Brandon explained. "He was just playing. Is my mom going to be okay?"

"I think so. We haven't lost a mom to a doghouse yet."

Jessica sighed, her body tensing at the sudden sound of a power saw.

"You're not going to cut her in half, are you?" Brandon asked, awe in his voice. "I saw them do it once on TV."

"Now, that's an idea. What do you think, Bill?"

"A little messy, but you're the boss, Reid. Whatever you think."

"Nah, the chief probably wouldn't like it."

"Would you just get me out of here?" Jessica snapped, her discomfort rising when the firefighter's hand pushed against her side. The rough calluses of his palm felt cool against her hot skin. "What are you doing now?"

"Relax. I'm just trying to see if we have any room. There's no opening, so we'll cut the wood from the top down in a semicircle, and see if we can't rip the piece off around you. Just try to be still, okay?"

"I'm not going anywhere."

"Keep your head down. We'll have you out in no time."

Jessica squeezed her eyes shut and offered a

silent prayer as the saw cut into the wood well above her body but close enough to send a few doubts through her mind.

As the pieces of wood were pulled off, she drew in clean, fresh breaths of air, suddenly realizing how little oxygen there had been in the doghouse. Finally, she felt a hand on her back, pulling at the wood until it gave, and she slithered out with relief.

Sitting back on her heels, she stared into a pair of smiling blue eyes that sparkled against tanned skin and sun-streaked brown hair. The man in front of her was well built with strong, muscular arms and a broad chest. Self-consciously, her hand crept up to her dark-brown hair, as she tried to calm her tangled waves into some semblance of order.

He smiled approvingly. "Good, you're still in one piece. Are you hurt anywhere? Do you want me to check you out?"

He leaned over and put his hands on her shoulders, and she immediately tensed. There was mischief in his eyes, along with something else—something that she hadn't seen in any man's eyes in a very long time.

Desire.

She shivered at the thought.

His fingers ran down her arms to her elbows and then lightly clasped her wrists.

"Feels good to me," he muttered.

She drew in a deep breath as an echoing response rushed to her lips.

Stopping those words from coming out, she pulled her hands away from his and jumped to her feet. It was then that she noticed the stricken expression on Brandon's face.

His mouth was shaking as he tried to stop himself from crying. Lifting a finger, he pointed an accusatory hand at the firefighter.

"You broke my doghouse," he said, sobbing the words out.

The man stared at the little boy somberly. "I did, didn't I? I'm sorry. It was the only way I could get your mother out."

"My dad made it for me, and now it's broke."

"Maybe he can fix it," the firefighter suggested.

"He's not here. He's in Boston."

"It's okay," Jessica interrupted, putting her arm around Brandon's shoulders. "We'll get a new doghouse. Although, we don't really need one. Wiley likes to sleep with you."

"But Daddy gave this to me. It's special. It can't be broken."

"Why don't we talk about this later, Brandon?" Looking at the firefighters, who were taking in the scene with interest, she smoothed down the line of her skirt, trying to regain her sense of dignity. "Thank you for helping me. I really appreciate it. I don't know how else I would have gotten out of there. I hope I didn't take you away from something more important—like a fire. Please, don't let me keep you. I'm fine now." She hugged Brandon as he started to cry. "It will be all right. We'll get the house fixed, don't worry."

As the firefighters left, Jessica let out a sigh, feeling completely drained, and her day hadn't even started yet. She squatted down in front of Brandon. "I'm sorry, sweetie."

"I don't like it here," Brandon said. "I want to go home."

"This is our home now."

"No, it's not."

"It's going to be fine, you'll see."

For a moment she thought she had convinced him. His shoulders stopped trembling, and his body seemed to relax in her arms. Then he lifted his head and stared at her with watery eyes.

"Maybe Daddy will come here to fix the doghouse for me," he said hopefully. "He could fly out on the airplane and then it wouldn't take so long to get here."

Jessica felt a stab of pain at the plea in his voice. Kevin wouldn't be coming to Half Moon Bay, and he certainly wouldn't be interested in fixing a doghouse he had only bought to annoy her.

"He's working, Brandon."

"He could take a vacation. This is a good place to come. We could go to the beach together and build sand castles."

His innocent words filled her with emotion. There would be no more building of sand castles with Kevin—not for her, not for Brandon. Kevin had taken all of their dreams and smashed them like a tidal wave hitting the beach. One day Brandon would know the truth about his dad, but that day would not be today.

"Come on, sweetie. We need to get to school." She paused, looking around the yard. "Now, where is that dog? I want to make sure he stays out of trouble while we're gone."

"He's probably hiding under your bed," Brandon said, a reluctant smile hovering on his lips. "He likes your fuzzy slippers."

Her eyes rounded at the thought. "He better not touch my slippers. Not if he knows what's good for him."

"He's just playing, Mom. He's my buddy."

Jessica shook her head, knowing she was beaten. Her slippers were probably in a dozen pieces by now, but at least Brandon had a friend. She would figure out the rest later.

Two

Morning recess was just ending when Jessica walked up the steps to Crestmoor Elementary. She dropped Brandon off at his second-grade classroom, taking a quick minute to explain his tardiness, then hurried to her own room down the hall.

When she opened the door, the noise level was extremely high and Donna Anders, the principal's admin, who had filled in for her, was trying to mediate an argument at the puzzle table between two of her most rambunctious boys.

"Oh, thank goodness, you're here," Donna said. "Now I know why I'm an admin and not a teacher."

"What's going on?"

"He took my pieces," Mitchell said.

"You took mine first," Robbie countered.

"That's enough," she said sharply. "If we don't share, we don't play. Remember?"

Both first-graders gave her angry, unhappy nods.

"Take a seat on the carpet. We're going to do story time in a minute."

Donna looked at her in amazement as the boys

immediately followed her instructions. "Impressive, Jessica."

She shrugged. "No big deal. Thanks for covering for me."

"What happened?"

"I had a problem with the car," she lied, hoping the doghouse story would never come out. "It's all good now."

"Great. I will happily leave you to your class." Donna turned, then paused. "Oh, by the way, Mrs. Standish volunteered you for the Community Emergency Certification Training class on Friday night. The fire and police department are co-hosting a two-session class for community leaders and every school is sending two teachers."

"Yes, she told me I would be doing it. She thought I would be perfect," she said dryly.

"And she didn't want to do it," Donna said, meeting her gaze. "She's been here for thirty years, and she's the most senior staff member here, including the principal, so she thinks she runs the school. She loves to give new teachers, especially, young, pretty and popular teachers, a hard time."

"It doesn't matter. I'm happy to take the training. It's just two nights, and since we're new to the community, it will help me get a better handle on things."

"It's good you see it that way. Some women would find better things to do with their Friday nights, especially when they're single."

"I'm not single. I'm divorced. There's a difference."

"If you say so." As Donna headed toward the door, Jessica looked around her classroom and began rapping out a series of orders. "Kimberly and Chelsea, I want those blocks cleaned up and put back in the box. Michael and Emily, turn the chairs right side up and push them back against the table. Marissa and Peter, you're responsible for putting the books back onto the shelf. The rest of you put away whatever is in your hands and take your place on the carpet."

The children began to move in one accord. Jessica nodded approvingly. Time to get the day started. There were a lot of things in her life she couldn't control, but her classroom was not one of them.

Two days later, Jessica walked into the high school gymnasium for the Community Emergency Certification Training class.

The other teacher representing Crestmoor Elementary was Paula Cummings, a fourth-grade teacher. Paula was a short, curvy blonde with brown eyes and a friendly smile. She was also in her fifth month of pregnancy for her second child, so there was a decided bump beginning to show under her oversized sweater.

"Jessica," Paula said, waving her over to the benches. "I saved you a spot."

"Great." She sat down next to Paula and looked around the gym. "There are a lot of people here."

"They said they're expecting about fifty."

"I didn't realize it would be this big."

"All the community groups like to work together."

"That makes sense."

"Where's your son tonight?"

"After-school care is having date-night tonight, so I didn't have to look for a babysitter. He's having pizza and watching a movie and is happy as can be."

"That's great, but wouldn't date-night be better if you were actually on a date?" Paula asked with a laugh.

"I suppose, but I don't know too many people in town."

"I should introduce you to some of my husband's single male friends. They would love you."

"Probably only until they found out I have a seven-year-old kid," she said dryly. "It's a game-changer."

"The right man won't care about that."

"So far, that man hasn't shown up." As she finished speaking, the mingling crowd settled onto the benches as several men in uniform walked through the door: two from the police department and two from the fire department.

Her heart skipped a beat as her gaze settled on a tall, fit, attractive man with light-brown hair, blue eyes, and a wide smile. It was the firefighter who had cut her out of the doghouse. Of course, he would be teaching the class, because apparently it wasn't time for her to live down that embarrassing episode yet.

"Oh, my," Paula whispered. "Good-looking men in uniform are definitely going to make this class more interesting."

The other firefighter, who had also been at her house, was handsome, too, with dark-brown hair, brown eyes, and an olive complexion. But he didn't draw her attention the way the other man did. As his blue-eyed gaze turned on her, she felt an unexpected jolt of desire.

Surprise flared in his eyes, followed by appreciation, and a slow, almost intimate smile. Butterflies danced through her stomach, and she swallowed hard.

"Do you know him?" Paula asked.

"Uh, I've seen him before, but I don't know him," she replied.

Luckily, the man stepped up to a microphone so she didn't have to answer any more of Paula's questions.

"Good evening, everyone. Thanks for coming. I'm Reid McAllister. This is Bill Carlton. We're from the Half Moon Bay Fire Department. Joining us is Mark Holmes and Ron Davenport from the police department. Later in the evening, we'll also have a representative from Mercy Hospital lead a discussion relating to emergency medical care. We have a full night planned, but we want to start out by letting you know how much we appreciate your interest and efforts to make our community safer." Reid paused, looking over at the other firefighter. "Bill is going to start things off."

As Bill began to discuss the different emergency situations that might occur in town, Jessica's gaze drifted to Reid, who seemed just as interested in staring at her as she was at staring at him.

She forced herself to break eye contact. She needed to focus on why she was here and that wasn't because of the sexy firefighter who'd seen her at her worst. Well, maybe the doghouse wasn't her *worst* moment, but it had been embarrassing. She flushed at the thought of what she must have looked like with her ass hanging out of the doghouse and her skirt hitched up around her thighs.

After discussing protocols and emergency procedures for fires, earthquakes, tsunamis, toxic hazards, and active shooter situations, the speakers moved from general information to more specific details, and over the next two hours, Jessica learned a great deal about how the community would respond to each of those situations. While she was trained in CPR and knew a lot about how to deal with school emergencies, it was eye-opening to see the broader picture of how a natural event like an earthquake could impact everyone.

At the end of the evening, the group was divided in half to role-play an explosion at a large city building. Jessica was put into the group of civilian responders while Paula was in the group of victims. They were given a few minutes to study their roles, the background of the situation, and the protocols they needed to follow. Then it was time to get to work.

Jessica was given three patients and was instructed to triage them according to the severity of their alleged injuries.

As her victims finished studying up on their injuries and got into position, Reid joined her. "We meet again," he said with a smile.

"Quite a coincidence," she replied, the nervous butterflies back in her stomach. It was ridiculous to be so affected by him. They weren't on a date. This was a professional moment. He was a teacher tonight, and she was a student. She needed to remember that.

"How did you end up here tonight?" he asked.

"I'm a teacher at Crestmoor Elementary School."

"And you pulled the short stick?" he asked with a grin.

The man had a smile that warmed her all the way to her core. "Something like that. But it's been very informative, and I do like to be prepared in case of emergency. So it's all good." She paused. "The other morning, I—I wasn't at my best."

"When I show up somewhere, I don't find many people at their best," he said dryly.

"But how many do you find stuck in a doghouse?"

"I have to admit you were the first one for that. But it doesn't even make the top ten of weird calls."

"I'm happy to hear that, because it's near the top of my list for embarrassing moments."

"It shouldn't be—you have great legs."

She flushed at his compliment. "I don't think you're supposed to say things like that."

"I'm definitely not supposed to say things like that, or notice things like that," he agreed with a smile. "Don't tell on me."

How could she possibly tell on someone who was as sexy and charming as Reid McAllister was?

"But let's get down to business and see what you've learned," he said, nodding his head to her first victim.

"Okay." She knelt down next to a middle-aged man who was playing the part of a forty-year-old unconscious male, bleeding from a head wound. She consulted her notes. "He has a bad head injury. He's unconscious, but he is breathing. I don't see any other visible signs of trauma, but obviously a head injury could be extremely serious. I would tag him as…" She consulted the list of five colored tags and the notes behind each decision. "Red."

"So he requires immediate attention and is a first

priority for transport to a medical facility?" Reid asked.

"Yes."

He nodded approvingly. "Good job."

She moved on to the next patient, and Reid followed along. The older woman was playing a teenager, who was conscious and sitting up with evidence of a broken arm, with a protruding bone.

"This person has an arm injury, but appears to be alert." She turned to the victim. "What's your name?"

"Catherine," the woman said. "I'm in a lot of pain."

"Do you hurt anywhere else besides your arm? Can you get up?"

The woman nodded. "I think so. It's just my arm."

Jessica looked over at Reid. "She's responsive. She knows who she is. She can walk. She would be marked with a yellow tag—her condition is stable but she needs care for her arm so she should be transported after the more seriously injured individuals." She paused. "Or would she be green? She could go to her own doctor and not go to the hospital?"

"Her condition says a bone is protruding through her skin."

She winced at that description. "Which sounds really painful."

"It also probably requires surgery, so that would keep her in the yellow group. If she had what appeared to be a sprain, her condition would go down to green."

"I can't believe I'm making any of these decisions," she said, standing up again. "I have no idea what's going on inside their bodies. What if they have internal bleeding?"

"You won't know. You have to make a trained observation based on the protocols."

She moved on to her final victim. Paula was sitting in a chair, but she was playing a nine-year-old, having trouble breathing, blood coming from her nose.

"I think this is severe," Jessica said, reading through the symptoms. "It's a child. The blood from her nose could indicate internal injuries."

"I can't—can't breathe," Paula said breathlessly. "I don't know where my mom is. I'm scared."

"It's going to be okay," Jessica told her, putting her hand on Paula's arm. "We're going to take care of you." She glanced back at Reid. "The breathing problems suggest urgent care since there could be a problem with her lungs. So she gets the red tag."

"Thank goodness," Paula said. "I was afraid I was going to get the black tag."

The black tag was for individuals that they couldn't save. Jessica frowned at the thought of having to put that tag on someone, especially if they weren't dead yet. "I don't think I could do it," she said to Reid. "How could I mark someone who's still alive as no hope? There's always hope, right?"

"Not always," he said seriously. "If this person was the only person at the scene, then, of course, you would work on them forever and get them to help. But this is a situation with potentially fifty plus victims. If a responder spends too much time on someone who can't survive, that person might cause someone else's demise. Instead of losing one person, you might lose two or more."

She shuddered at the thought. "I really hope I

never have to do this."

"We all do," he said.

"Are you done with me?" Paula asked. "I need to leave a few minutes early. I have a babysitter who has to be home by nine fifteen."

"You're good," Reid said. "Thanks for coming. Will we see you next week?"

"Absolutely," Paula replied. "I'll see you tomorrow, Jessica."

"You two know each other?" Reid asked as Paula moved away.

"Yes. Paula is also a teacher at Crestmoor."

"What grade do you teach?"

"First grade."

"You have little ones."

"Yes. I like that grade. They're not quite as dependent on me as kindergartners, but still intensely curious and eager to learn."

"Is your son in your class?"

"No, he's in second grade, and I would never be his teacher. I think it's important to have a separation there. I'm sure at some point he'll hate that I'm even a teacher at his school, but right now he likes knowing I'm just down the hall, especially since it's a new school. We moved here around Christmas." She had no idea why she'd just told him that. "Don't let me keep you if you need to work with another group."

"I think everyone is covered," he said, glancing around the gym. "How do you like Half Moon Bay?"

"I love it. I actually grew up on the other side of the hills in Palo Alto, so I wasn't totally unfamiliar with the area."

"Where's your son tonight?"

"The after-school care at Crestmoor offers a date

night once a month on Fridays, so Brandon is hanging out there."

"And you're not on a date? Where's your husband?"

"My *ex-husband* lives in Boston."

His eyes sparked at that piece of information. "Ex-husband, huh?"

"Yes."

"For how long?"

"Six years. And you ask a lot of personal questions, Mr. McAllister."

"Please, call me Reid. I'm a curious person. Do you have some secret past you don't want to talk about?"

"No, it's actually fairly boring."

"Let me be the judge."

"Fine. Long story short—I grew up in Palo Alto, but I've been living in San Diego the past few years. I came back at Christmas because my mom has been having some health issues, and I wanted to be closer to her. No big secrets, just family stuff."

"I'm sorry to hear about your mother."

"Thanks."

"How's your son dealing with the destruction of his doghouse? I felt bad about that. It looked like it meant a lot to him."

"Brandon will be fine. His father sent him the doghouse along with the dog a few months ago—without asking me first, I might add."

"It doesn't sound like you were too happy about it."

"I love dogs, but I have my hands full working a full-time job and raising Brandon on my own. Kevin knew I was going to move, so adding a puppy into the mix was a crazy idea. But he presented both to Brandon while I was out, and by the time I arrived home, Brandon was in love with the dog. I couldn't say no, which is, of course, what Kevin was counting on. He got to be the hero and I got to pay the price." She hated that she sounded so bitter. She'd had plenty of time to get over Kevin, and she had, but sometimes the anger about his irresponsibility just got the best of her. "I'm sorry. You don't want to hear all this."

"Actually, I'd like to hear more. Do you want to get a coffee, Jessica? There's a place not far from here. I'm assuming you might have a little time before date-night is over?"

"You're asking me out?" she asked in surprise.

"It's just coffee. Maybe dessert. What do you say?"

She didn't know what to say. She actually couldn't remember the last time a man had asked her out. It had been at least a year. She rarely put herself in situations where someone would ask her on a date. She was always with Brandon, or working, or at home.

She should say no. It was crazy to say yes. Dating with a child was complicated. *So why was she so tempted?*

"It really doesn't need that much thought," Reid added. "The place is two blocks away. We can walk there. You can leave whenever you want."

"I—I can't," she said, feeling an instant wave of regret. "I'm sorry. I have to go. We're done here, right?"

"Until next week," he said. "Just so you know, I'm disappointed."

She was disappointed, too, but she couldn't tell

him that. She handed him her clipboard. "I'll see you next week." Grabbing her bag and jacket, she headed out of the gym before she could change her mind. Reid McAllister might not think coffee was a big deal, but instinctively she knew it was, because she hadn't felt such a pull to a man in a very long time. While that might be a good thing, it could also be very bad. She'd put Brandon through a lot of changes in the past couple of months. The last thing she needed to do was bring a man into the picture.

She was doing the right thing, she told herself firmly, as she got into her car. She was choosing safe over potentially sorry. But as she drove away from the school, she couldn't help feeling like she'd just missed out on something wonderful.

Three

The ocean was brutally cold even with a wet suit on, but Reid wasn't worried about the weather, only about finding the perfect wave to ride into the shore. He'd been out since seven a.m. and it was almost eight now. Clouds swirled overhead, and there was a brisk wind whipping off the water, but that just made the waves better.

Surfing was his favorite way to start the day, and weekends were usually busy off Pillar Point. Today there were at least ten other surfers on the water, most of them in their teens, with a few thirty-somethings like himself mixed in. Age wasn't a factor on the ocean; it was all about desire. He'd been surfing since he was twelve years old, and while he seemed to get out less often these days, he still tried to hit the beach at least a couple of times a week.

Looking over his shoulder, he saw a wave beginning to develop. Two other surfers nearby were readying themselves for the same ride. He waited for just the right moment, then began to paddle, picking up speed as a wall of water built up behind him.

He moved onto his knees, then his feet, feeling an incredible sense of exhilaration as he battled the sea, keeping his balance as his board cut through the powerful white water.

For a split second in time, he felt on top of the world.

But as the wave crashed onto the shore, he lost his balance and plunged into the water. Just like that, the second was gone.

The ocean pounded him down to the beach, punishing him for having thought for even an instant that he could win. Eventually, his knees scraped along the sand, and he breached the surface of the water, sucking in a long, deep breath of salty air. He found his board bobbing a few feet away. He grabbed it and walked out of the water, his heart still pumping from the wild ride.

He wasn't surprised to see his friend and coworker Bill Carlton on the beach, tossing a stick to his Golden Retriever, Oscar, who raced in and out of the sea with wild abandon. Like himself, Bill had an apartment only a few blocks away from this stretch of sand, and in the past they'd often surfed together on their days off. But since Bill had moved in with his girlfriend, that didn't happen as often as it used to.

"Nice ride," Bill commented. "For a second, I thought that kid was going to beat you, but he wiped out before you did."

Bill was talking about the tattooed, long-haired blond teenager named Connor, who'd become a regular at the beach the last few months. While Connor and his friends sometimes made him feel like an old man, he respected their skill and their daring. "Connor is good, but not as good as me," he retorted.

Bill laughed. "Gotta love the fact that old age has not made you humble, Reid."

"I'm thirty, not ready for the retirement home."

"So, listen," Bill began, a thoughtful look on his face.

Reid suddenly had a feeling their chance meeting was not so much by chance. "What's going on?"

"I got a call from Larry Hendricks."

"Your friend in Chicago?"

"Yes. He told me there's an opening at his firehouse. It's on the south side, rough neighborhood, but if you want to apply, he'll put in a good word for you. He said they've had a revolving door of firefighters the last year, and the guys across town don't want to work there."

"You're really selling it," he said dryly. He'd been thinking about making a move to a big city for a very long time. Family circumstances had prevented him from doing that before now, but those circumstances were about to change.

"Just giving you the facts. Larry said the firehouse is strong, good guys, so it's not all bad."

"How soon do they want someone?"

"May. Apparently, the latest hire is transferring out then, so you have some time to think about it."

"May could be perfect. Tara graduates in June. As long as I can make her graduation, it could work out."

"But it is in Chicago. There aren't any ocean waves there, Reid. All they've got is a big lake. And don't forget the bitter cold in the winter, the killer wind chill, and the hot summers."

He smiled. "I don't think anyone is going to make you a spokesman for the city, Bill."

Bill shrugged. "It wouldn't be my choice."

"No, it wouldn't. It would be mine." As he gazed out at the sea, he thought he would miss this town, this view, but he'd spent his entire life in Half Moon Bay, and he'd wanted to live somewhere else for as long as he could remember. He'd been trapped in this town, in this life, but he was about to be free. "I could adapt," he said, looking back at Bill.

"I'm sure. If you want to apply, it's on you."

"Thanks for letting me know."

"I still hope you won't go for it. We've got a good squad. I hate to see that get messed up. It's not easy breaking in a new guy."

"You'd manage. I've been waiting for Tara to graduate for a long time. Once she's legally an adult and on her own, I don't have to feel guilty about leaving her behind. She'll have her own life."

"I get it. But just because you can do something doesn't mean you should."

"Where did you read that? On a fortune cookie?"

"I'm serious, Reid. You made that promise to yourself when you were a teenager. You have a lot more to give up now than you had then. You have a life here."

He did have a life, and it wasn't a bad life, but was it the one he wanted? Didn't he need to find out for sure?

Bill picked up the stick and tossed it down the beach to Oscar. "So what's up with you and the beautiful brunette from the doghouse?"

"Nothing, unfortunately. I asked her for coffee. She said no."

Bill grinned. "Strike one. That doesn't happen to you very often. But maybe it's a good thing. She has a kid and a dog."

"And an ex-husband," he added. "But they were divorced six years ago, so it's not like she's on the rebound."

"Still, that's a lot of baggage for someone like you. You like to travel light."

"Normally, I would agree, but there's something about Jess…I don't know exactly what it is."

"She's very attractive."

"It's not just that, though. I'd like to get to know her better."

"If she's been divorced six years, she must have split from her husband when the kid was a baby. He couldn't have been more than seven or eight."

"Yes," he said, thinking about that. *What had gone wrong so fast?* Jessica clearly had some anger toward her ex, but he was in her life enough to add a dog and a doghouse into the mix, so it wasn't like he'd completely disappeared.

"What are you going to do? You'll have an opportunity to see her again next week. You can give it another shot."

"I'm not sure I want to wait that long."

Bill tilted his head, giving him a speculative look. "What's your plan?"

"Not completely sure. I'm still working on it."

"Want to talk about it over breakfast?"

"No. I'm going to go back out. I think better out on the water."

"It's getting rough out there."

"I can take it."

"Well, don't do anything stupid. Leave that to the teenagers."

He laughed as he grabbed his board. "I will do that."

He *was* doing something stupid, Reid thought, but he wasn't on his surfboard anymore; he was standing outside Jessica Blake's house just before eleven on Saturday morning.

He didn't normally—make that ever—get involved with people he'd rescued, especially not divorced women with kids. As Bill had said, that was way too much baggage for him. He had enough problems to deal with in his own family; he didn't need to take on someone else's problems.

Dating for him was fun, easy, and mostly forgettable. Which was why he really shouldn't have come here.

But he couldn't get Jessica out of his head. It wasn't just the memory of her curvy, sexy body hanging out of the doghouse, or her thick, wavy brown hair that would look great spread across his pillow, or her dark-brown eyes that were intelligent and curious and sometimes sad and angry, too; it was also the sweetness he saw in her smile when she wasn't looking at him, the strength in her shoulders and the determined lift in her jaw when she'd told him no, she couldn't see him.

He wasn't used to hearing no; Bill was right about that. He found himself wanting to change her mind. And he didn't want to wait a week to have the chance to do that.

Along with Jessica, her son's heartbroken face had also gone around in his head. He'd had to destroy the doghouse to get Jessica out, and it had obviously torn her son apart. He understood that, especially now that he knew the kid had gotten the dog and the house from his dad, someone he apparently didn't see that often. He knew a lot about disappointing fathers. He couldn't fix that, but he could fix the doghouse. And if he could do something about it, he should.

Of course, Jessica had to let him in the door first.

He grabbed his toolbox out of his Jeep and walked up to her front door.

He hadn't noticed much about the house during their call, but now he could appreciate that the yard was neatly landscaped and well-tended, a garden basket filled with wildflowers hanging from an awning over the porch. It was another sign of how hard Jessica was working to make a good life for herself and for her son.

He rang the doorbell, and a moment later, he was looking into her surprised face. She'd obviously been cleaning, her hair up in a ponytail, thick, yellow vinyl gloves on her hands and some dirt running across her cheek.

Despite the fact that she didn't have on an ounce of makeup and her faded jeans and tank top were obviously work clothes, her beauty hit him like a punch to the gut. Her skin was clear and creamy, her eyes bright, her lips pink even without lip gloss.

Her brown eyes widened as she said, "Reid, what are you doing here?"

He held up his toolbox. "I came to fix the doghouse."

"That's not necessary."

Her words were interrupted by the excited barks and sudden appearance of a big black Lab, who took a happy leap toward Reid.

"Down, Wiley," Jessica said, trying to grab the dog's collar.

"It's okay," he told her. "Hey, buddy." Wiley barked in enthusiasm.

"He's not dangerous, just very friendly," she said.

"I can see that."

He set down his toolbox and gave Wiley a scratch around his ears as the dog barked and licked his face. "I take it this is the wallet thief."

"Yes, it is."

"I can see why you needed the big doghouse."

"He won't fit into it in another month or two. He's only eight months old. Apparently, he's going to grow a bunch more."

"I love Labs. They're friendly and great with kids."

"They are."

"Who is it, Mommy?" Brandon asked, ducking around in front of his mother to give Reid a surprised look. "Hey, you're the firefighter who broke my doghouse."

"And today I'm going to fix it," he said.

"You are?" Brandon asked, his wary expression turning to a hopeful smile.

"If your mother agrees." He turned his gaze on Jessica.

"You have to let him fix it," Brandon told his mother.

"The front is torn apart," she said, giving him an annoyed look. "I'm not sure it's fixable."

"I have some wood in my truck. I think I can rebuild it for you," he said. "It may not be perfect, but it will be better than it is now. It's the least I can do—since I broke it." He knew he was putting her in a bad position, but if he was going to get another chance to get to know her, this was his best opportunity.

"We don't blame you for breaking the doghouse," Jessica said. "You did what you had to do to get me out. Brandon knows that."

"Still, it won't take much time. What do you say?"

"Please, Mommy?" Brandon put in.

"Of course," she said with a helpless shrug. "You're very generous to offer, Reid. Come in."

"Yay!" Brandon clapped his hands as Reid stepped over the threshold.

Wiley barked again with excitement, and Reid laughed, thinking it had been awhile since anyone had responded to him with so much enthusiasm, although Jessica obviously didn't share Brandon or Wiley's attitude.

"Can I help you?" Brandon asked him.

"Absolutely," he said.

"Sorry for the mess. I was just cleaning," Jessica said.

He didn't see much of a mess, just a little kid clutter in the small, cozy house. As she took him down the hall, he noted the photographs of Brandon that covered the walls. She was in some of them, but he didn't see any of Brandon's father.

When they entered the kitchen, he was assailed by the delicious aroma of chocolate cookies. "It smells good in here," he commented.

"We made cookies earlier."

"Maybe I could get one of those," he said hopefully.

"Let's see how you do with the doghouse first," she replied, with a sparkle in her eyes, for the first time letting down her guard just a speck.

"Pressure," he said.

"I have a feeling you're used to pressure; in fact,

you probably love it," she added, as they went through the small adjoining family room into the backyard.

"I don't mind it," he said. "It keeps life interesting."

As soon as Wiley hit the grass, he took off, barking at a squirrel making its way across the back fence. Then he stopped to sniff the roots around a tree before making another run around the yard.

"He has a lot of energy," Jessica said.

"I can see that. Does he actually use the doghouse?"

"Only to hide things he steals from the house."

"Mommy, he's just playing," Brandon put in. "It's hide-and-seek to him."

Reid laughed, thinking it was hard to argue with Brandon's logic. Jessica just rolled her eyes and turned back to him.

"So what do you think?" she asked.

As he perused the broken doghouse, he had to admit the damage was worse than he remembered, but it was mostly the front and top pieces that had been torn apart. He could put it back together. It might not look as good as new, but it could work. He'd spent a lot of off-days working construction for one of the guys at the firehouse. He might not be able to handle a house remodel, but a doghouse shouldn't be too difficult.

"I can fix it," he said confidently.

"What can I do to help?" Jessica asked.

"Nothing. I have some wood in my truck. I'll go get it."

"You can go out through the gate. Just make sure Wiley doesn't go with you."

He smiled. "Or I'll be going on a run, right?"

"He does love to run," she agreed.

"Got it."

She gave him a somewhat awkward smile and then turned to her son. "Brandon, I'm going to finish cleaning inside. You stay in this yard. No going out front, okay?"

"Okay."

"Just send him into the house if he's too much trouble," she told Reid.

"He won't be."

She gave him an uncertain look. "I really don't know why you're doing this."

"It's part of the job," he lied. "We're a full-service fire department."

"I doubt that, but thanks."

"You're welcome. And I'm going to hold you to that cookie offer."

"I'm sure you will," she said, giving him one last thoughtful look before heading into the house.

Four

An hour later, Jessica had changed into clean jeans and a soft deep-purple sweater, run a brush through her hair, and put on some makeup after being appalled by the sight of her dirty face in the bathroom mirror. Then she'd headed to the kitchen to cut up fruit, make tuna fish sandwiches and put some freshly-baked cookies on a plate. She'd actually accomplished quite a bit, considering she'd looked out the window every five minutes to see what was going on in the backyard.

Moving back to that window, she pulled the curtain aside to see what progress had been made since her last viewing. She was surprised to see that Reid was almost done, which was a good thing. That meant he'd be gone soon.

On the other hand…she wasn't quite ready for him to leave. As he leaned over the doghouse to hammer in a nail, she could see the muscles in his back working against the thin material of his T-shirt. He was obviously athletic and fit enough to be a firefighter, but it wasn't only his hot body that made her palms sweat. It was also the blond streaks in his light-brown hair that glowed in the sunlight, the shadow of beard along his masculine jawline, his incredible blue eyes, and the great laugh he had when Brandon accidentally hit him in the back with a soccer ball. Her son had apparently lost interest in the building project.

Reid didn't get mad when the ball bounced off him. He just grinned and said something to her son, who laughed in return and then kicked the soccer ball toward Wiley, who barked and ran after it, happy to be in the game.

She felt a rush of emotion at the scene—happiness, but also sadness. She'd imagined this kind of scene with Brandon and his dad a thousand times. For the first year or two of Brandon's life, she'd thought Kevin might change his mind and realize he couldn't walk out on his son, or on her, but that had been the foolish and desperate thought of a young woman way over her head in single motherhood.

Kevin had never wanted to be married to her. He'd just tried to do the right thing for as long as he could stomach it. And he'd never wanted to be a father, either. She thought he loved Brandon in his own way, but that way was distant and disconnected.

Brandon deserved a dad who would show him how to grow into being a man, who would hang out with him on a Saturday and kick a ball around with him and his dog.

But that man wasn't Reid, she told herself firmly, realizing how quickly her thoughts were getting away from her.

She'd made a promise to herself a long time ago that no matter how difficult it was to be a single mom, she would not marry again for any reason except for love—real, genuine, life-lasting love. And that man would not only feel that way about her but also her son. She wouldn't settle for less, and she wouldn't be with someone just to get Brandon a father. She'd already messed up once. She wouldn't do that again.

And while Reid was being an awfully nice guy, her gut told her to be careful, to go slow. It wasn't just about her making another mistake; she also didn't want to expose Brandon to more potential heartbreak. He had enough of that every time his hopes were dashed when his father didn't keep a promise or didn't show up.

She had to keep her standards high.

Letting the curtain fall, she leaned back against the nearby wall and closed her eyes, drawing in several deep breaths, hoping to settle the fluttery feelings running around inside her. It was one thing to be logical and practical and demand the best, but what about emotion, what about love, what about sex?

She was lonely. She missed being with a man, not just physically, but emotionally. She missed having not just someone she could count on, but someone who could make her laugh, someone she could tease and just have a good time with. But she hadn't had much luck in the dating world the few times she'd tried it.

One guy had seemed good on the surface, but his interest in her son had quickly faltered when he realized she really wasn't just going to go to bed with him because he'd taken Brandon to a baseball game.

Frowning, she hoped that wasn't what Reid was doing now, fixing the doghouse and being nice to her kid so she'd go out with him.

Cynically, she thought that probably was the reason. Why else would he be here after she'd said no to coffee the night before? He wanted another chance with her.

It was flattering, but it also made her feel nervous.

The back door flew open, making her jump in surprise.

Brandon and an exuberant Wiley came in first, followed by Reid.

Despite her determination to keep things cool, her heart skipped a beat when his blue eyes met hers. She felt like she was looking into the deep, dark sea. And there was a good chance she could drown there. She drew in a breath. Her guard wall was going to need some heavy-duty reinforcing.

"The doghouse is fixed," Brandon told her with a happy smile.

"It's not as good as new," Reid said. "But it will shelter Wiley if he ever chooses to go inside, which, to be honest, doesn't seem too likely."

She smiled. "I agree, but now he has the option."

"I also made the opening a little wider, just in case you need to go looking for something."

She flushed at the reminder. "I appreciate that. I have your cookies, but I also made lunch if you're interested. It's nothing fancy, just tuna sandwiches and fruit."

"Sounds good to me."

"Great. Brandon, why don't you go upstairs and wash your hands and take that shirt off? Were you rolling around in the dirt?"

"Wiley knocked me over," Brandon said.

"It's true," Reid put in. "I saw it happen."

"I believe you. Just get cleaned up."

"Okay."

As Brandon left the room, Reid moved toward the kitchen sink to wash his hands. She gave Wiley a treat, happy when he settled down on his blanket in the family room. Apparently, he was tired out—at least for a few minutes.

She grabbed the sandwiches off the counter and took them to the table, then sat down. Reid joined her a moment later.

"Everything looks good," he said with a smile. "Especially those cookies."

"We have a rule in this house—dessert after the meal."

"Got it. You're tough," he said with a grin.

She couldn't help but smile back at him. "Not that tough, trust me. If I were, I probably wouldn't have made cookies at all and just stuck to healthy snacks."

"What's wrong with a little flour, butter, sugar, and chocolate chips?"

"Pretty much everything you just said, but warm chocolate chip cookies are my downfall."

"Really?" he asked, giving her a speculative look. "So those are your Achilles' heel?"

"So to speak. But don't get too worked up. I won't do just anything for a cookie."

He laughed. "Good to know."

"You don't have to wait for Brandon if you're hungry."

"I'm in no hurry. It's nice to talk to you."

As his gaze settled on her face, she felt the need to turn the conversation away from herself. "So, have you always lived in Half Moon Bay?"

"I've been here since I was six. Before that, we

were in San Francisco. I actually went to elementary school at Crestmoor."

"Really? I'll have to look for you in the old pictures in the attendance office."

He laughed. "Please, don't."

"Why not? I bet you were a cute kid. Is your family still here?"

His smile dimmed a bit. "My mother and sister are. My dad took off a long time ago, so I know a little something about fathers disappointing their sons."

She wondered if that was partly behind his offer to rebuild the doghouse. "How old were you when he left?"

"I was six when he took off the first time. That's when my mother brought me here to Half Moon Bay. Her sister lived here, and she let us stay with her for a while. A couple of years later, when I was ten, my father came back. He got a job as a teaching pro at the golf course and he stuck it out for two years before deciding to take off again—right after he got my mother pregnant with my sister. Since then he's only shown up every few years."

"I'm sorry."

He shrugged. "It is what it is."

"So he's a golf pro?"

"Sometimes. In reality, he's probably more of a con man. He's the kind of guy who is funny and charming and everyone likes him, but no one really knows where he makes his money. He does teach golf, and he has worked at a lot of clubs around the country. He's also done some real-estate investing with some of the country club people he plays golf with. Only a small amount of that money ever seems to come back to my mom and my sister, however."

"What does your mother do?"

"She's an assistant manager at a florist right now. She's recently gotten into a lot of holistic hobbies—meditation, yoga, painting, who knows what else? She changes jobs as often as my dad does." He paused. "I know it was hard on her to get over him, but I just wish she and my sister would stop waiting for him to come back, for some miracle to happen, but they just can't seem to stop imagining some moment where he'll show back up and tell them he loves them and wants to make them happy. My mother gave him a million chances to be a husband and a father. He just isn't cut out for it."

"I guess you always want the person in your heart to be the actual person in real life, but unfortunately, it doesn't always work out that way."

"That's true." He paused, tilting his head as he gave her a curious look. "Do you want your ex-husband back?"

She took a breath at the blunt question. "You get right to the heart of things, don't you?"

"Just want to know where your head is at."

"No. I don't want him back."

"Not even for your son? That's why my mother took my father back. She said it was for me. She wanted him in my life. But that wasn't the real reason. She wanted him with her. Like you just said, she wanted him to be the guy of her dreams."

"My situation is different. Kevin and I met in college. I got pregnant my senior year, and we did the right thing by getting married. But neither of us were ready for marriage or a child. When Brandon was a year old, Kevin said he was done. He couldn't do it anymore."

"I can't believe he left you with a baby."

"It shocked me, too. But in reality, even when he was with me, he wasn't with me. I honestly don't even know why I ever thought I loved him." She paused, realizing how deep their conversation had gotten. "Anyway, he's not in my life, and while I would like for him to show up for Brandon, that doesn't happen very often. What hurts the most is watching Kevin disappoint Brandon."

"I get it. I was always bothered more by my sister's tears than my own feelings. She's had a hard time accepting that her father doesn't really care about seeing her."

"You said you were twelve when she was born, so she must be a lot younger."

"She's turning eighteen in a little over a week, and she'll be graduating from high school in a few months. I can't quite believe it. Tara is amazing, a really great kid—young woman," he amended. "She keeps telling me to stop calling her a kid, but that's how I see her."

She could see the fondness and brotherly pride in his eyes. "She must be thinking about college."

"She is. She got accepted to San Diego State; she's heading down there in the fall. I can't quite believe it."

"That's a great school. When we were in San Diego, I met a lot of alumni from the university; they all loved it."

As she finished speaking, Brandon came back into the room and sat next to Reid.

"I'm starving," he said.

"Then let's eat." She passed the plate of sandwiches to Reid, then put some fruit on Brandon's plate, telling him the cookies would come after he finished his lunch.

Over the meal, Brandon kept up a steady stream of conversation, bouncing around from subject to subject. Reid somehow managed to keep up with it all, asking questions and laughing at Brandon's juvenile jokes.

"You shouldn't encourage him," she told Reid after Brandon told a particularly silly story.

"It was funny," Reid said without apology. "Trust me, I've heard worse at the firehouse."

"I want to be a firefighter when I grow up," Brandon announced.

She looked at her son in surprise. "When did you decide that?"

"When Reid got you out of Wiley's doghouse. It was cool. I want to put out fires, too. Reid said I could come to the firehouse one day."

"If it's okay with you," Reid put in. "And, of course, you're welcome, too."

"When can we go, Mom?"

"Uh, I don't know. We'll figure it out."

"I'm on duty Monday. You can come by after school," Reid suggested.

"Can we go, Mom? Can we?" Brandon asked.

"That sounds like a possibility." She didn't really want to commit to more time with Reid, but Brandon's desire was hard to resist.

"Can I ride on the fire engine?" Brandon asked Reid.

"You can sit on it. But we won't be taking it out."

"Oh, okay. Can I turn on the siren?"

"How about the lights?"

"I guess. Do you have a pole to slide down?"

"No," Reid said with a laugh. "But we have a lot of other cool stuff. I'll show you when you come." He paused. "What are you guys doing this afternoon?"

"We're going down to the beach to collect seashells," Brandon said.

She frowned, having totally forgotten she'd promised to do that.

"Great idea. It's a nice day for that. The clouds have cleared since this morning. It's a lot warmer now than when I was out surfing."

"You surf?" she asked in surprise, immediately picturing Reid bare-chested, in sexy swim trunks.

"As often as I can. I grew up on the water."

"It's fairly rough around here, isn't it?"

"Not that bad unless there's a storm coming. Did you ever surf in San Diego?"

She laughed at that question. "No, I never even considered it. I'm a good swimmer, but the ocean scares me. It's so powerful."

"And there are sharks," Brandon put in. "Have you seen a shark, Reid?"

"I have not. Fortunately, they don't come around too often. Surfing is fun. It's challenging, exhilarating—"

"Terrifying," she put in.

"No risk, no reward."

"That's a much easier attitude to have when you're a single guy and not a mom with a kid," she couldn't help pointing out.

"Can you come with us to the beach?" Brandon asked Reid.

Reid glanced over at her. "I could come along, if that's all right with you."

She hesitated, then decided she needed to answer

that question without Brandon listening. She turned to her son. "If you're done eating, why don't you run upstairs, and grab a sweatshirt and your bucket and pail, and whatever else you want to take to the beach, okay?"

"Okay. I hope you can come," Brandon said to Reid, and then ran out of the room.

Reid turned his penetrating gaze on her. "I feel a *no* coming in my direction."

"I don't want you to get the wrong idea, Reid."

"And what would that be?"

"That I'm interested in going out with you. I'm not." She felt like a liar at the end of that statement, but it had to be said.

"Well, that's direct."

She swallowed hard. "It's not that you're not attractive—"

"Or that you don't feel the chemistry," he finished, a knowing gleam in his eyes. "But you're afraid. You don't like to take risks."

"Not when my son is the person who could get hurt. We don't even know each other, so this shouldn't be a big deal."

"It's just a walk on the beach, Jessica. Do you really think we're going to fall for each other over seashells?"

His teasing question made her feel like an idiot. "When you put it like that—no. But why waste your time on someone who just told you she's not interested?"

He leaned forward. "Because you are—and so am I."

A little shiver ran down her spine at his words. The air between them sizzled with anticipation. If she leaned forward, she could kiss him.

No! What was she thinking? She couldn't kiss him. She'd just told him she wasn't interested in him.

Her thoughts had barely finished forming in her brain when Reid leaned over and touched his mouth against hers. The heat was searing, but the kiss was over way too fast.

"Just thought we should get that out of the way," he said lightly.

She stared back at him in bemusement. "I can't believe you just did that."

"And I can't believe you told me you weren't interested."

Before she could reply, Brandon came into the room, with his bucket and pail in his hands. "Are we going now? Is Reid coming?" he asked. Wiley jumped up and barked, adding his plea into the mix.

Three males—all waiting for her to say yes…

It was just an afternoon at the beach as Reid had said. *What could possibly go wrong?*

Five

After a brisk walk on the beach, Jessica sat down on the sand while Brandon and Reid took turns throwing a tennis ball to Wiley, who happily moved between the sand and the sea.

The wind gusted, and she drew her thick sweater more tightly around her body. While it was bright and sunny, there was a brisk breeze and a fog bank drifting closer to the shore with each passing minute. The Northern California beaches were definitely more rugged than the ones she'd left behind in San Diego. The ocean current was stronger, the beaches rockier, and the landscape a bit more wild.

Because it was mid-February, there weren't too many people on the beach, a few body surfers, an older couple walking hand-in-hand along the shoreline, two women and several kids having a late afternoon picnic, and a group of teens attempting to launch kites into the air.

She wished she'd thought about getting a kite. It was a good day for it. But as she heard Brandon's laugh ring out, she smiled, thinking that right now, a tennis ball, a sandy, wet dog, and a man giving her son plenty of attention was all any of them needed. For the first time since she'd moved Brandon away from his home and his friends in San Diego, she felt like things might be okay. They could be happy here. They would make more friends and they would have more days like this.

She wasn't quite sure that Reid was having as much fun as she and Brandon were, although he seemed to be. He was a carefree, easygoing kind of guy. She didn't think he worried about too much. He seemed easily able to adapt to whatever situation he was in and to embrace it for what it was. She liked that about him. She also liked that he could relate to Brandon's situation. Maybe that's why he was being so nice. Reid's father had left when he was young, and he knew what that felt like.

But as she saw Brandon give Reid a look of hero adoration, she also knew that her son was falling fast and furiously for Reid, and that could be a problem.

She hadn't expected to deal with this kind of situation so soon. She certainly hadn't been looking for a man, but here was a really good one—handsome, sexy, funny, happy…

Her hand crept to her mouth, her lips tingling at the memory of their quick, hot kiss in the kitchen—something else she hadn't expected. Reid certainly didn't waste time. He went after what he wanted, and she was both flattered and terrified that he seemed to want her.

But that couldn't happen.

Actually, it probably wouldn't happen.

Reid might enjoy playing with Brandon, but she doubted he really wanted to date someone who was divorced and had a child. He probably just hadn't thought it through that far. But she didn't have the luxury of living minute to minute; she always had to consider the future, not just her future but also Brandon's.

Still, as Reid had said, it was just an afternoon at the beach; she couldn't let herself get too far ahead.

A few minutes later, Reid came over and sat down next to her. "Your kid and your dog have a lot of energy," he said with a laugh, his cheeks red from the wind, his blue eyes sparkling.

Her gut clenched with a sharp, stunning jolt of desire that stole her breath for a second.

Reid must have seen something in her face, because his gaze darkened. "Jess?" he said softly. "What are you thinking?"

"Nothing," she lied.

"Sure about that?"

He held her gaze for a moment, then she forced herself to look away.

Brandon was picking up seashells, a good thirty feet away from the water, and Wiley was digging in the sand next to him, so they were happily occupied. She wouldn't have minded if they were a little closer; then she could have used them as a buffer for a conversation she didn't want to have.

"Jessica?" Reid repeated.

She turned back to him. "Thanks for playing with Brandon."

He frowned. "You have to stop thanking me for hanging out with you. It's not a chore. Although..." He paused, tilting his head. "If you want to show your gratitude, I can think of something better than words. In fact, I believe our all-too-brief kiss was what you were thinking about a second ago."

"I don't know what you're talking about."

"Yes, you do."

She saw the teasing light in his eyes. "You like to shake things up, stir the pot, don't you?"

"Only when the pot is as pretty as you are."

"That's a terrible line."

"It sounded better in my head," he admitted. "You're too serious, Jessica. You need to loosen up."

"I'm loose. I mean," she amended quickly, "I'm not that serious. I can have fun. I'm here, aren't I?"

"You are—at least physically. But I feel like you're carrying a lot of weight on your shoulders."

"I'm a single mom. I have a lot of responsibilities and a lot of worries."

"Like what? What's at the top of your worry list?"

She shook her head. "You don't want to hear about all my problems."

"How about one?"

"Brandon is always at the top of the list. I've been worrying about him since before he was born. I was only twenty when I got pregnant, twenty-one when he was born. Sometimes, I feel like we're growing up together, and I'm not sure that's a great thing."

"He's a good kid, Jessica. He's funny, caring and respectful. From what I can see, you've done a lot right. And it sounds like you've done it on your own for a very long time."

She appreciated his words more than she could say. "He is a good kid. I just don't want to screw him up."

"I think screwing your kids up is part of being a parent," Reid said with a laugh. "They have to have something to blame you for."

She smiled. "You're right. Heaven knows, I blame my parents for a lot. And now I feel guilty for saying that, because I'm sure they did their best."

"My parents didn't come close to doing their best. It wasn't just my dad who went in and out of my life; my mom was good at disappearing, too. She gets on these kicks and throws herself into them with complete obsession, completely forgetting everyone else in her life. My sister's eighteenth birthday is a week from tomorrow, and it's a fairly important milestone, but my mom decided that instead of being here for that, she had to go on a yoga retreat to India with her new Yogi guru or whatever you want to call him."

"Wow, India, huh?"

He nodded. "She read that book several years ago, the one where the woman goes to different countries to find herself. She said she was inspired. Since then, my sister has spent a lot of time sleeping on my couch or staying with her friends while our mother is seeking enlightenment."

"Maybe it will make her a better person."

"That's an optimistic viewpoint."

"So what are you doing for your sister's birthday?"

"I told her I'd take her to dinner, but she didn't sound excited about it. I think her exact answer was…*whatever*."

"She probably wants to do something with her friends."

"I said they could come."

"Dinner with your brother might be good when you're twelve, but eighteen…" She shook her head. "You need to plan something fun that she'll really like."

"Got any ideas?"

She thought for a moment. "What about a spa day for her and some of her friends—your treat?"

"That's an idea. Where do you do that around here?"

"Lots of places. The Ritz Carlton has an amazing spa. I'm actually going out there tomorrow to have lunch with some girlfriends. We're not getting massages, but the restaurant is good, too. I think your sister would like it."

"So I should take myself out of the party and just fund it."

"Does that disappoint you?" she asked.

He grinned. "Not even a little."

"I didn't think so. Where is your sister today? Is she staying by herself?"

"No, she's staying with her best friend. At least that's the story she gives me. I'm a little concerned that she might be staying alone in the house, but I can't be with her every second. With my job, I'm away for several nights at a time. But I have to trust her. She's never gotten into trouble."

"Then you should trust her."

"Mom, look what I found," Brandon interrupted, showing her a huge shell on his outstretched sandy palm.

"That's amazing," she said.

"I found some other ones, too." He handed her the shell so he could reach into his pocket and pull out more of his treasures.

"Good job, Brandon. These are great."

"I'm going to get some more," Brandon said, dumping the shells into her lap, then running back down the beach with Wiley barking in accompaniment.

"What are you going to do with all those?" Reid asked.

"I have no idea," she said, as she put the shells in Brandon's bucket. "Some kind of art project probably. We have another two dozen shells at the house. I'll figure something out. Maybe I can turn it into a math project."

"You're thinking like a teacher."

"And a mom with too many seashells," she said dryly. "Brandon loves to collect things."

"He's lucky you encourage that. My mom would have dumped those shells in the trash first chance she got."

"I would never discourage curiosity. That's what childhood is all about."

"Or should be. Did you always want to be a teacher?"

"I did. I used to play school when I was growing up. I'd make my little brother be my student until he refused, and then I had to make do with my stuffed animals. I'd line them up in chairs and give them lessons. They never talked back and always did what I said. Well, not always. Sometimes one of them fell out of their chair and I had to give them a time-out."

He smiled. "You were very strict."

She laughed. "I was. I liked being in control of everyone and everything around me back then, and I still do."

"Your classroom is your castle and you're the queen."

"That's about right. What about you? Was it always the firehouse for you?"

He gave a negative shake of his head. "No, I had dreams of being an internationally renowned surfer for a very long time. The year after I graduated from high school, I hit the road and traveled around the world to surfing competitions."

"I didn't realize you were that good."

"I had my moments."

"What did you do for money? Did your parents support your adventure?"

"Not even a little bit. I saved up money while I was in high school. I did any odd job I could find, from construction to lawn mowing and dog walking. Once I left home, I picked up work and money wherever I could find it. I didn't need much, and I slept on a lot of couches as well as in the back of a car when I had to."

His words were vivid and filled with light and she could almost see him as a young man, barefoot, in swim trunks, dragging his surfboard from one ocean to the next. "You loved it, didn't you?"

"It was a great time of my life. I saw some amazing parts of the world."

"I'm surprised you ever came home."

"I had to. About six months after I left, my mom was hospitalized after taking almost an overdose of medication. She wasn't trying to kill herself; she was just anxious and stressed out. I don't think either of us realized how much I was doing for her and Tara until I was gone. A social worker told me they were concerned enough about Tara's welfare that foster care might have to be an option. Tara was only eight years old. I couldn't let that happen."

"So you came home," she said, impressed with the maturity he'd shown.

"Yes, and I went to college and then decided to become a firefighter. One of my best friends, Bill Carlton, was going that route. You met Bill the other night."

"Of course."

"Bill's dad was a firefighter, so he was on the inside track. It took me an extra couple of years to get there, but eventually I did."

"And I assume your mom got better once you were back in town."

"She did, for the most part. She still had her moments, but I was here to pick up the slack. I promised her I'd stay until Tara was grown."

"You're almost there," she murmured.

"Almost."

She thought about that for a moment. "Do you have any regrets about cutting your surfing career short?"

"I don't believe in regrets. And I love being a firefighter, so it all worked out."

"Are you ever scared? I can't imagine running into a burning building or any of the other things you do," she said, thinking there was definitely another side to the fun-loving Reid. "The other night at your class, it really hit home to me the kind of situations you deal with all the time. I hope I'm never called into action."

"You probably won't be, but if you are, you'll be ready."

"I hope so. The class was very informative."

"I'm glad." He paused. "So, tell me a little about your family, Jess. Are your parents together?"

"They are. My father is a doctor, and my mother has gone from homemaker and PTA president to helping run community fundraisers for the hospital and the community where they live."

"Are you close to them?"

"I'm geographically close now, but emotionally—not so much," she admitted. "My parents always had busy lives, and my younger brother and I were scheduled out with activities as little kids. There was a lot of emphasis on achievement. Whenever I spoke to my father, it always seemed to be about my grades or what classes I was taking. And my mom and I weren't much closer. But it was all pretty fine until I got pregnant and ruined my life," she said with a sigh. "Their words, not mine."

"They don't really think that, do they?"

"Oh, yes, they do. They were marginally happy when I married Kevin but then disappointed again when we got divorced. I can't ever seem to do anything right. But my little brother makes up for me. He's in his third year in medical school, so he's following in my dad's footsteps, and making him very happy."

"Your parents should be proud of you, too. You must have finished college and gotten your teaching credential while taking care of a baby by yourself."

She liked hearing the annoyance in his voice, knowing that he was on her side. "I did get my credential after Kevin left. I went through those days in a haze. The divorce made me realize that I had to take care of Brandon. I couldn't be dependent on anyone else. So I became a teacher, and it's been good, because I've had access to daycare and I get the same holidays and hours as Brandon, so it works pretty well. Plus, I like teaching, so it's a win-win."

"You're amazing, Jess."

"Not really. Just doing what I have to do," she said. "And Brandon is worth it. He's my life. I want him to have the best of everything."

"I think he already does. He has you."

Reid's quiet words, his warm gaze on her face, made her feel admired in a way she hadn't felt in a very long time.

Reid wasn't just good for Brandon; he was good for her, too.

As a gust of wind lifted her hair again, she shivered, realizing the sun was sinking lower in the horizon. They'd been at the beach for over two hours. "We should probably go," she said somewhat halfheartedly, not really wanting to leave, but it was getting cold.

She stood up and called for Brandon.

As he came running in her direction, followed by Wiley, she said, "Thanks for coming with us, Reid."

"I told you to stop using that word. I was thinking we should stop at Caffe Romano and get some coffee for us and hot chocolate for Brandon. Have you been there yet?"

"No, but I've driven by. It looks charming."

"A friend of mine runs it. The coffee is excellent."

"I do love coffee, but we have Wiley."

"They have heaters on the patio. We can sit outside with the dog. This is a dog town."

"I have noticed that," she said.

"Then what do you say?"

Since she found it impossible to speak the word *no* where Reid was concerned, she said the only thing she could say. "Yes."

He probably shouldn't have suggested coffee, but Reid wasn't ready to say good-bye to Jessica, and he had a feeling that as soon as this day ended, Jessica would find a way to put up her guard and push him out of her life.

There was a part of him that thought that might be a good thing. She wasn't the kind of woman he normally went after. She had a lot of baggage with Brandon and Wiley and an ex-husband, and considering the amount of drama he had in his own family, he usually tried to avoid finding it elsewhere.

But her big, dark-brown eyes got to him along with her pretty face, and her beautiful soft lips that he wanted to kiss again and again. He felt like he was taking a ride on a wave that could very well crush him, but he couldn't turn back now. If this ended in a hard landing, he'd deal with it.

As they walked into the patio of the coffee house, he saw the owner and his friend, Steven Talmadge, bussing a table. At six foot five, Steven was a tall, skinny, thirty-three-year-old with brown hair and green eyes.

"I thought you were the boss," Reid said with a laugh.

"Which means I do everything," Steven replied.

"This is Jessica, her son Brandon, and their dog Wiley," he introduced. "Steven Talmadge. He used to make coffee and cake at the firehouse. Now he makes it for the whole town."

"Nice to meet you," Steven said. "I just turned on the heaters. If it's not warm enough out here, let me know."

"It feels great," Jessica said, as they sat down at a table.

"I'll bring some water for Wiley while you decide what you'd like," Steven added. "Menus are on the table, but I have to tell you that Dee made a couple of incredible pecan pies this morning, and we only have a few slices left."

"That sounds good to me," he replied. "Jessica?"

"I'm going to stick with coffee."

"I want pie," Brandon said.

"It's too close to dinner," she told him.

"But Mom—"

"I'll tell you what—you can have whipped cream in your hot chocolate, and if Reid wants to share a bite of his pie, I won't say no."

Brandon gave Reid a questioning look, and he laughed. "You've got it, buddy," he said.

"I'll also take the Italian roast," Jessica told Steven.

"Same for me," he added.

"You got it. Coming right up," Steven said, then headed into the café.

Jessica glanced around the patio. "This is lovely. I like the way the ivy wraps around the white fence and there's a partial view of the water."

"Steven had his eye on this place for a while. It was originally a deli, and he does serve salads and sandwiches if you want anything more substantial to eat."

"No, this will be fine," she said, turning her gaze back to him. "You said Steven used to be a firefighter?"

"Yes. He was injured on the job two years ago, and he wasn't able to come back to active duty, so he and his wife Dee decided to go after another dream they had to open a coffeehouse."

"How bad was his injury?"

"Bad enough that it took him about a year to rehabilitate."

She frowned at that piece of information. "Well, I'm glad he's all right now."

"Me, too."

"Do you think you'll always be a firefighter?" she asked curiously.

"I can't imagine doing anything else."

As he finished speaking, Steven returned with their drinks and a slice of pecan pie, which he put in the middle of the table, along with three forks. "Just in case you want to try it, too, Jessica," he said.

"Thanks. It does look amazing."

Another waiter brought out a bowl of water for Wiley, who happily lapped it up, then laid down next to Jessica's chair, obviously worn out from the beach.

"This is good," Brandon said with a happy, whipped-cream smile.

Reid laughed. "Looking good there, Brandon."

"Use your napkin, honey," Jessica said. Then she picked up her fork and took a bite of the pie. "Wow, excellent," she murmured.

"And you didn't want pie," he teased, taking a bite himself. "Dee did herself proud. This is delicious."

"Can I have some?" Brandon asked.

"One bite," Jessica told him. As she finished speaking, her phone buzzed, and she pulled it from her bag to read a text.

"Everything okay?" he asked.

She set her phone down. "Yes, sorry. I've been waiting all day for a reply from my friend, Maggie, about whether we're on for tomorrow, and she was just getting back to me."

"Is Maggie another teacher?"

"No, she's a college friend. She works at a hotel in Napa. But we're having lunch together tomorrow at the Ritz Carlton."

"She's coming a long way for lunch."

"It's a pre-wedding lunch for my friend Isabella. She and her fiancé are getting married in about eight weeks—this is actually the second time they've postponed it for a variety of reasons, but it looks like the date is now certain, and we have to plan a shower, a bachelorette party, and make sure our bridesmaid's dresses fit. Lots to do and lots to talk about."

"Sounds like fun." She nodded, but there was a shadow in her eyes. "Although, you don't look too excited," he added.

"No, I'm excited. I love to see my friends."

"But…"

"But," she admitted, "the weddings have been a little crazy the last two years. This will be my fifth bridesmaid's dress, and I'm fairly sure number six is not too far behind."

"Really? That's a lot of weddings. Can't you say no? Just be a guest instead of a bridesmaid?"

"No, absolutely not. I'm the reason my friends made a pact that we would always have a wedding party, and we would always show up, no matter where we were and what we were doing."

"What do you mean? Why are you the reason?"

"Because I got married at a courthouse with no bridesmaids, and they were all furious at me. I met these women freshman year of college. We were in the same dorm, and we became really close friends.

We were always there for each other, but when I hurriedly decided to marry Kevin, I just ran off and did it. A couple of them showed up at the courthouse because they found out about it, but they were disappointed I hadn't included them. Anyway, after that we made a pact that our weddings would be special no matter the circumstances, and that we'd all be there for each other."

"Then it looks like you're going to be in more weddings."

"I just wished they were a little more spaced out for the purposes of my budget, but everyone is falling in love at the same time. I'm really happy for them."

Despite her words, he heard something else in her tone. "But…" he repeated.

"Why do you keep saying that?"

"Because you aren't being completely honest."

"I am. I'm ecstatic for my friends."

"But you feel a little bit on the outside," he said, venturing a guess.

She sighed. "I guess I do. The weddings are all beautiful, but they remind me of…" She paused, glancing over at Brandon, then back at him. "Decisions I've made," she said vaguely.

He understood she didn't want to talk about her failed marriage in front of her son.

"I get it."

"The good thing is that Brandon gets to be a ring bearer again, and he loves that."

"I get to wear a tie," Brandon said with a smile. "And I carry the rings on a pillow."

"Sounds like fun," he said.

"Were you ever a ring bearer, Reid?" Brandon asked curiously.

"Nope. I've never been in a wedding. A couple of friends have gotten married, but I thankfully wasn't asked to be in the wedding party. Tuxedos aren't really my thing. I'm not big on formal wear."

"What about when you get married?" Jessica asked.

He laughed. "I have no idea. I've never thought about it."

"Never?"

"Not even once."

"Interesting," she mused.

He realized that never having thought about getting married probably wasn't going to put a checkmark on the positive side of the list Jessica had going in her head about him. But he didn't want to get into a discussion about that now. Neither, apparently, did she.

"We should get going," she said.

He nodded. "I'll go inside and settle up the bill."

"Can I pay for something?" she asked.

"Not a chance." He went into the café and settled up with Steven, then headed into the parking lot where Jessica, Brandon, and Wiley were waiting by the car.

As he drove them home, he wished he could think of some way to prolong the evening, but he'd probably already pushed his luck by inviting himself along on the beach trip. He was usually more than ready to call a halt to a first date, but with Jessica, he had the feeling that if he said good-bye to her, it might be for the last time.

A few minutes later, he pulled up in front of her house. Brandon was impatient to get into the house to use the bathroom, so Jessica handed him the keys. As Brandon and Wiley went inside, she lingered by the car door.

"I know you don't like the word," she said with a small smile, "but thanks for today—for everything: the doghouse, the beach, the pie."

"It was fun—all of it. Although, next time you and Brandon will have to get your own piece of pie."

"That's a fair point." She drew in a deep breath. "Good-bye, Reid."

"Let's not call it good-bye."

"We should. You're going to complicate my life, and I'm going to complicate yours."

"That's looking at the glass half-empty."

"I'm just being a realist."

"You told Brandon you'd bring him to the firehouse on Monday."

A frown furrowed her brow. "I forgot about that."

"He'll be disappointed if you call it off."

"He will be," she agreed.

"So we'll see each other then."

"I guess we will, but after that—"

"We'll figure out what comes next," he said, cutting her off. "No need to decide now, is there?"

"I don't want you to get the wrong idea."

"I have a lot of ideas already," he said lightly.

She flushed at his comment. "Bad ideas."

"Bad, wrong—who knows? Let's find out."

She let out a sigh. "I'll see you Monday with Brandon at the firehouse. That's all I'm agreeing to."

"That's all I'm asking."

She shut the door and headed to the house. He watched her until she got inside and then muttered to himself the two words he'd been hesitant to say in front of her: "*For now.*"

He knew Jessica was going to complicate his life,

but he hadn't felt this intrigued and involved and curious to know more about a woman in a very long time, and he wasn't going to let a seven-year-old and a dog scare him off.

Six

Maggie was the first one Jessica saw when she walked into the Ritz Carlton on Sunday afternoon. She was a few minutes late, having had to wait for the teenage girl who lived across the street to come over to watch Brandon. Fourteen-year-old Hayley had babysat once before and had gotten along well with Brandon, so hopefully everything would go well for a few hours. But she was close to home if there were any problems.

Maggie was standing by the fireplace in the lobby, talking on her phone, but when she saw Jessica, she gave her a wave and motioned her over.

Jessica smiled to herself, thinking that the strawberry-blonde, blue-eyed Maggie looked even prettier and happier today than she normally did. There was a rosy shine to her fair skin and a sparkle in her eyes that had been there ever since she'd fallen in love with Cole Hastings last October. She expected their engagement announcement to come any day now, maybe even today.

She'd always been the closest to Maggie. They'd

shared a room her senior year in college until she'd had to drop out to marry Kevin. Maggie was the one who'd first found her crying on the floor of the bathroom with a pregnancy test in her hand. She hadn't asked any questions; she'd just wrapped her arms around her and given her a hug. She'd really needed that hug.

Liz had come in next: practical, no-nonsense, get-down-to-business Liz, who'd insisted she go to the doctor just to make sure she really was pregnant. Both Maggie and Liz had made her feel that no matter what happened, her friends would have her back.

The rest of the group had been just as supportive: Andrea with her optimistic *don't worry this will change your life in a good way attitude*; Julie with her quiet, caring, and diligent delivery of crackers to ease morning sickness; Isabella, who had encouraged her to keep dancing and exercising through it all; Laurel, who'd dropped off books on pregnancy and motherhood; and Kate with her motherly nurturing, who'd given her the support she'd wished her own mother would give her. They'd all been there for her.

Now, it was her turn to be there for each of them.

"Sorry," Maggie said, as she got off the phone. "That was my assistant manager at the Stratton. A water pipe broke and flooded one of our guestrooms. Everyone is in a tizzy."

"I had the same problem at my new house. It was a nightmare for a while."

"You didn't tell me about that."

"Well, there was nothing you could do. I dealt with it—as you are doing now."

"Yes. Fortunately, we have plenty of empty rooms this weekend since it's off-season, so we should be able to get everything repaired without displacing anyone. Enough about that. It's good to see you," Maggie said, giving her a hug.

"You, too. How is your job now that you're the hotel manager? And more importantly, how are things with Cole?"

Maggie's smile grew bigger—if that were possible. "The job is good. It's taken me a few months to grow into it, but now things are running smoothly. But I don't know how long I will be there. Cole and I found another property in Napa with a small vineyard and a big old house that would make a perfect boutique hotel. We're thinking about buying it. Cole would like to make wine, and I've always wanted an inn where I can really get to know the guests. Not that I don't love the Stratton. It's amazing, and Cole's aunt has given me so many opportunities there."

"But this would be something for you and Cole to build up together. It sounds wonderful. Does this mean you're going to think about having a wedding soon?"

"Yes, it does." She held up her hand to show off a beautiful oval-shaped diamond. "He actually asked me a few days ago."

"Oh, Maggie, I'm so happy for you. I knew Cole was the right guy for you the first time I met him at the baseball game."

"He is pretty great," Maggie admitted. "We have so many plans. It's fun to really have a partner. And he's awesome enough to put up with my family. Actually, he was responsible for bringing us together at Christmas, something I couldn't seem to make happen on my own."

"So are you telling everyone today?"

"I am. We don't have a date yet, but we're thinking September. I've mentioned it to Kate, but no one else knows yet."

"I won't spoil it. You can make the big announcement. I'll start putting money away for another bridesmaid's dress."

"I'm going to make sure they're not hideous."

"That I would appreciate. Kate is certainly making a lot of money as a wedding planner off this group alone."

"I know. I told her she better make room in the schedule for me, although I'll probably have something small and intimate up in Napa. I don't need anything big and grand."

"You might feel differently once you start planning." She paused as a pretty brunette with dark hair and blue eyes came rushing into the lobby. Kate was always like a whirlwind. When she was in the room, there was a new energy level.

"How late am I?" she asked.

"Later than me," Jessica said with a smile. "But I just got here, too. We should head down to the restaurant. I'm sure everyone else is already there."

"I just told Jess about the big news," Maggie said to Kate.

"Oh, good," Kate said with a laugh. "I'm terrible with keeping secrets; I can't wait till all our friends know. I also can't wait to start planning your wedding."

"You never get tired of weddings, do you?" Jess asked.

"I really don't. Some are more stressful than others, but there's nothing better than helping someone on such a happy day."

"Hopefully, their happy days last longer than mine did," she said, instantly killing the mood. "Oh, sorry, forget I said that."

"No, you don't have to apologize," Maggie said. "You have every right to be cynical."

"But I don't need to bring my cynicism to lunch. So it's gone. Let's get back to happy."

"One day you will have another special day," Kate said. "And many more happy days after that, Jessica. You just need to find the right man."

"Well, that's certainly true, but I'm not exactly looking. I'm busy with Brandon and my new life."

"How has the move gone?" Kate asked, as they walked down the stairs to the restaurant.

"Well enough. Brandon is settling in at school, and so am I."

"I'm glad you're closer," Kate said. "How is your mother?"

"She's doing her treatment, and it looks like everything should be all right in the end."

"That's great news," Maggie said. "I'm sure she likes having you only a half hour away."

"We'll see. In my family, sometimes distance is a good thing." She paused as Maggie gave Isabella's name to the hostess, who escorted them to a window table with an amazing view of the ocean.

Andrea, Julie, Liz and Isabella were already seated and engaged in rapid-fire conversation, which tended to be how all their gatherings went.

After a round of hugs, she sat down between Maggie and Kate and glanced across the table at Andrea, a beautiful blue-eyed blonde with a zest for adventure and a passion for truth-telling. As a journalist, Andrea loved to shake things up. "Where's your sister?" she asked Andrea, referring to her twin sister Laurel, who was the only one of their group who wasn't present.

"She's at a birthday party for her mother-in-law; she couldn't get out of it. But she said to say hello to everyone."

"That's too bad." She smiled at Isabella next. Isabella was a dark-eyed brunette with olive skin and a passion for dancing. She ran a dance studio where she'd met her soon-to-be husband, Nicholas Hunter. "How is the bride-to-be?"

"A little crazed," Isabella replied. "But Kate is keeping me calm when she's not driving me crazy with wedding questions."

"I hear that," Liz put in. "Kate is the best, but she will make you consider every last detail."

"So it's perfect," Kate said defensively.

"My wedding was certainly perfect," Julie said. "And so was yours, Liz."

"I'm just teasing," Liz said.

Liz and Julie had gone to high school together and had been friends long before they'd gotten to the dorms. While they were similar in that they had varying shades of blonde hair, they were opposite in personality. Liz was a sharp, quick-witted, somewhat cynical woman who never failed to state her opinions and Julie was a quiet, determined, idealist who worked very hard to make a difference in the world through non-profit fundraising.

"So you live the closest, Jessica; you should have been the first one here," Liz pointed out.

"You're right. I had to wait for my babysitter, whose basketball game ran late."

"How is Brandon?" Julie asked. "Has he settled in

since your move?"

"Pretty much. He's starting to make friends, so that's good. He likes that we're still near a beach, although the Half Moon Bay beaches are a lot colder than the ones in San Diego."

"That's true, but they're beautiful," Julie said, waving her hand toward the window. "Sometimes I forget how close I am to the beach when I'm in San Francisco, surrounded by tall buildings."

"Well, you're always welcome to come down and visit," she said.

"Okay, first order of business is Isabella's bachelorette party," Liz said. "I was thinking either a weekend getaway or maybe just a day of pampering and shopping and eating and drinking in San Francisco."

Jessica held back the sigh that wanted to push past her lips. The bachelorette parties were always the most difficult for her. She'd had to miss most of them, simply because getting a weekend away from Brandon was impossible.

"I was thinking a weekend in Carmel," Julie put in.

"Or we could go to Vegas," Andrea said. "Michael can get us suites at pretty much any hotel we want."

Andrea's husband Alex had made a fortune in the toy and video business, so Jessica was fairly sure any rooms he came up with would be first class.

"Vegas is always fun, but what about New Orleans or New York?" Liz suggested. "Just to shake things up."

"What do you want to do, Isabella?" Kate asked.

Isabella gave them a helpless look. "Honestly, I

don't know. Whatever we do together will be fun. I don't want anyone to go to too much trouble or have to spend a lot of money. We could just do dinner one night."

"Or you could all come to the wine country," Maggie said. "I can get you rooms at the Stratton, or we can drive up to Calistoga and do the mud baths."

"Ugh, mud is not my idea of a party," Liz said dryly.

Their conversation was interrupted by the arrival of a waiter with multiple champagne glasses on a tray. "I understand we're celebrating a wedding," the waiter said with a smile.

"Yes, this lovely lady," Andrea said, pointing to Isabella.

"Congratulations," he said. "The first round is on the house."

"Who did this?" Isabella asked, then glanced over at Kate. "Katie?"

Kate simply shrugged and smiled. "I think he said it was on the house."

"Sure it is," Maggie said dryly.

After the waiter handed out their champagne glasses, Kate said, "Let's have a toast. To our next beautiful bride, Isabella."

"To Izzie," they echoed, lifting their glasses.

Jessica took a happy sip of her sparkling liquid. She had a feeling she might need more than one glass to get through all the wedding talk.

As she set down her glass, she noticed that neither Andrea nor Liz had actually taken a sip. Andrea wasn't much of a drinker, so that wasn't completely surprising, but Liz had never been shy about tossing back champagne, especially for an occasion like this.

"So what do we think?" Liz asked. "Can we narrow down a location for the bachelorette party at least?"

"Hold on," she said. "Why aren't you drinking, Liz?"

Liz's jaw dropped. "Uh…I'm not thirsty."

"Andrea didn't drink, either," Maggie said, exchanging a quick glance with Jessica.

"So…" Julie asked as Andrea and Liz were put on the hot seat.

Andrea blushed. "Well, I don't want to make this day about anything but Isabella, but I do have some news. I was going to tell you later, but, here goes…I'm pregnant."

Andrea's news received a flurry of squeals and congratulations. Then all eyes turned to Liz.

"Do you have something to say, Liz?" Julie asked.

A smile spread across Liz's face. "As a matter of fact, yes! I'm pregnant, too. I'm almost three months. I didn't want to say anything too early. I didn't want to jinx it."

"I'm right behind you at eight weeks," Andrea said. "This is going to be great. Our kids can be best friends, too."

"I would love that," Liz said, her eyes blurring with surprising tears. "Damn these pregnancy hormones for making me emotional."

Jessica laughed. "The tears are the least of it. They can make you crazy, too."

"I can't believe this," Kate said. "Your bridesmaids' dresses are not going to fit eight weeks from now. We're going to have to have them altered."

Everyone laughed at Kate's worry about the bridesmaid's dresses.

"You'll make it work," Isabella told Kate. "You always do."

"Yeah, well you guys aren't making it easy," Kate replied. "I think someone else has a confession to make."

Jessica couldn't help glancing at Maggie. "It's time," she said.

"Okay, fine, I'm not pregnant," she said with a laugh. "But I am officially engaged. Cole and I are going to tie the knot."

Maggie's announcement was met with more happy replies and soon all three women were fending off dozens of questions about due dates and baby names and wedding plans. They only paused for a few moments to place their orders and then got right back into the conversation.

It was suddenly all a little too much for her. She pushed back her chair and headed to the restroom.

She didn't make it all the way there. The doors leading onto an outside terrace beckoned to her. What she really needed was fresh air and a minute to regroup. She was happy for everyone, but she felt a little overwhelmed, and she didn't really know why.

Looking out at the ocean, she realized she was lying to herself. She did know why; she just didn't want to admit it.

"Jess?"

She turned to see Maggie walking onto the patio. "I was just on my way back to the table," she lied.

"Sure you were. What's wrong? I know you didn't come out here to look at the view, since you can see it every day."

"It is beautiful," she murmured, knowing Maggie wouldn't be satisfied with the answer.

"Come on, Jess. What's bothering you?"

She really didn't want to answer that question. It would make her seem petty and childish and selfish.

"All right, let me guess," Maggie said. "It has something to do with Andrea and Liz being pregnant and me being engaged."

"I'm super happy for all of you."

"You don't look super happy despite the fake smile you're giving me. I thought you'd be excited two other people are joining your mom club."

She let out a sigh. "It hasn't been much of a club the past several years with just me in it."

"Well, it looks like it's growing quickly."

"I know. They have a lot to look forward to."

"So do you."

"Do I? Sometimes I feel like I've been standing in place while everyone else is moving forward, which doesn't make sense since I did everything first: I got married, I had a baby, I got divorced. But the last few years…" She ended her statement with a helpless shrug, then added, "It's just that all these weddings and now the pregnancy announcements—they just remind me of how many bad decisions I've made, and how I did everything out of order."

Maggie's brows drew together in concern. "There's no order. Things happen when they happen."

"Or when you're stupid and you let them happen before you're ready. I wish I'd made some of those big life decisions a little later and with more wisdom."

Maggie smiled. "Your life isn't over, Jessica. You can fall in love again, get married, have more kids. Just leave out the divorce part next time."

She appreciated Maggie's light words. "I plan on it. And I want you to know that I'm not talking about having Brandon. He's everything to me. I have no regrets that I had him."

"You don't have to explain, Jess. It's complicated, but that's what life is sometimes."

"True. Enough of this pity party. Let's go back to the table."

"Before we do that," Maggie said, her gaze more serious. "I just want to say it's okay to feel whatever you feel. None of us have walked in your shoes, and I think sometimes we're a little insensitive about things—like the bachelorette party. We don't want to leave you out by planning something you can't go to."

"But I don't want you to make plans based around me. I will try my hardest to come, but if I can't, I want Isabella to have the best bachelorette party ever."

"Well, let's see if we can't do both. I am glad you moved back to the Bay Area. I know I'm still a good hour and a half away from you, but at least you're closer to everyone else, and we can all see each other more often."

"I'm happy about that, too. And don't tell anyone else I was having a moment, okay?"

"I wasn't planning on it," Maggie said. "You know I always have your back."

"And I have yours."

Their food was just being served when they returned to the table, and the conversation continued to jump around as they discussed everything under the sun from babies, to brides, men and jobs. It was girl talk, and as much as some of it made Jessica uncomfortable, she also loved the depth of their conversation, the real friendship that they shared, and she was happy to give pregnancy and baby advice to Liz and Andrea. It would be fun to see all their worlds expand. And it would be nice to have someone else in her mom club as Maggie had called it.

As they paid the check, Kate turned to her and said, "Have you met anyone interesting since you moved here, Jess?"

"She means men," Liz put in from across the table.

Reid's image flashed in front of her eyes, and she paused a second too long.

"That's a yes," Andrea said, surprise in her voice. "And you haven't said a word about him."

"What's his name?" Maggie asked, a gleam in her eyes.

"There's nothing big to report. I might have had a conversation with a guy, but that's it."

"A good-looking guy?" Maggie inquired.

"Very," she couldn't resist saying. "He has light-brown hair with streaks of blond, a great tan, and the most amazing blue eyes. He's a firefighter."

"So he's got a great body," Liz put in.

"From what I've seen so far—I'd have to say yes."

"How did you meet?" Kate asked.

She was not about to share exactly how they'd met. "He's teaching a community class on emergency preparation, and I'm representing my school at the class."

"Did he ask you out?" Liz asked.

"Yes, but I said no, because I have a kid."

"You can still date," Andrea said.

"It's a lot more difficult when you have a seven-year-old. There are a lot of things to consider. Anyway, probably nothing is going to happen, so we don't need to talk about it."

"You should bring him to our annual pizza cook-off next Saturday," Andrea said.

"Yes, you should," Liz said.

"It would be fun," Julie agreed.

"And introduce him to all of you and your guys—I don't think so," she replied with a shake of her head. "We haven't been on a date, at least not just the two of us."

"What have you done together?" Maggie asked curiously.

"We went to the beach with Brandon. We had some coffee. That's it."

"Well, think about it," Kate said. "See how this week goes. And if you want to bring him, bring him."

"And don't forget, we have a teenager ready to watch Brandon and however many of his friends you want to bring," Andrea put in. "Alex's game room is a kid's dreamland. Trust me, Brandon will not be bored."

"It's really nice of you to do that."

"It's not a big deal."

"Well, thanks. Brandon will love it, and I probably will bring a friend along for him."

"Great."

She pushed back her chair. "I have to go. I only have the babysitter for another twenty minutes."

"You all have to stop at my car on the way out," Kate said, as they gathered their things and stood up. "I have the bridesmaid's dresses. I want everyone to try on their dress tonight and let me know what you think about the sizing. We'll probably have to make alterations closer to the date for Liz and Andrea, but now that I know that will be an issue I'll make sure to have a seamstress on call."

As they walked out of the restaurant, Maggie pulled Jessica aside. "I can't believe you held back that juicy tidbit about a hot firefighter."

"Don't make more of it than it is. Reid is a very attractive man who could get any woman he wants."

"Maybe he wants you. I'll make you a deal," Maggie said. "I won't make more of this if you won't make less of it."

"What does that mean?"

"It means give him a chance. Someday you're going to have to let someone else in. Maybe this is the guy."

A little shiver ran through her as she thought about Reid. *Was he the guy? Did she have the guts to find out?*

Seven

Monday afternoon, Reid checked his watch for the sixth time in about that many minutes.

"You have somewhere to go?" Bill asked, as he looked at him across the table in the kitchen of the firehouse. "Because our shift isn't over for another twelve plus hours."

"I know," he muttered, setting down the newspaper that he hadn't been able to concentrate on.

"Want to play some five-card draw?" Bill asked, shuffling the pack of cards in his hand.

What he wanted to do was see Jessica and Brandon walk through the door. It was a little after four, and they were supposed to come by after school. School had ended at three. Even if Jessica had had to work after that, it was still getting late.

Maybe they weren't coming. She'd made it pretty clear she didn't want to get involved with him or start something that might end up in complicating her life and hurting her son. But Brandon would be disappointed if she didn't bring him to the firehouse. Surely, she didn't want that.

"What is wrong with you?" Bill asked, giving him a speculative look. "You're more restless than you usually are. Is something going on?"

"No, just—bored," he said. "It's been a long, dull day."

"Considering our work, it's a good day, Reid."

"You know what I mean."

"Did you look into the Chicago job yet?"

"Not yet," he said tersely, wondering why he hadn't done that.

"I'm surprised you didn't get right on it," Bill said, raising a speculative eyebrow.

"You know, maybe I'll do that now."

Before he could act on that thought, the sound of a female voice brought him to his feet. He couldn't believe how happy he was to see Jessica and Brandon come through the door. She wore black jeans, boots, and a dark-purple sweater, her hair loose about her shoulders. Her beauty stole the breath out of his chest.

Jessica gave him a tentative smile as she came forward, while Brandon's excited grin spread from ear to ear.

"Hi, Reid," Brandon said, running over to him.

He caught him and swung him up in his arms. "I'm glad you made it," he told him.

"Mommy took forever," Brandon complained.

"He's right. Sorry we're late. My after-school meeting ran long," she said. "Is this still a good time?"

"It's a great time." He looked over at Bill and saw his friend smile as he got up to shake Jessica's hand, a knowing gleam in his eyes. "Do you remember Bill Carlton?"

"Of course. Hello again. I'm Jessica Blake. This is my son, Brandon. Reid kindly offered to show us around."

"Well, Reid is known to be *kind*," Bill said with a laugh.

"Can I sit on the fire truck?" Brandon asked.

"Absolutely," he said.

For the next hour, he showed Brandon and Jessica around the firehouse and introduced them to the other guys. He got more than a few sideways winks; he'd never asked a woman to come by the firehouse before, and he was going to get a hard time later, but he didn't care. It felt oddly good to share his work life with Jessica. Not that she was here for him. It was all supposed to be for Brandon.

As for Brandon, he was over the moon when he got to put on a helmet, try on Reid's big boots, and explore the fire engine. Reid had done a lot of tours with kids Brandon's age, but somehow this time felt different—personal.

"Thanks for the tour," Jessica said, as he put the gear away. "I know your dinner is almost ready, so we should let you eat."

"It will keep. I'm used to reheating food."

"Well, you don't have to do that tonight. I should get Brandon home. He has homework."

"I'll walk you out. Did you park in the lot?"

"I did. I hope that was okay."

"Absolutely."

They walked out to her car, and Brandon quickly hopped into the backseat. Jessica shut his car door, then turned back to him.

"Don't thank me again," he said quickly.

She smiled. "You should stop being so nice if you don't want to be thanked."

"I was nice, wasn't I?"

"Yes," she said a little warily.

"Instead of saying thanks, why don't you have dinner with me one night? How about tomorrow?"

"Tomorrow?"

"I know it's soon, but why wait? I'm off tomorrow, so it works for me."

She hesitated. "Uh, I don't know. I'd have to see if I could get a babysitter. I only know one girl who lives across the street, and she's pretty busy."

"Why don't you ask her?"

"I just don't think it's a good idea, Reid. This—whatever *this* is—it can't go anywhere."

"I just want to take you to dinner, Jess. There's a great Italian restaurant on Main Street. Best homemade pasta you'll ever eat. Do you like pasta?"

"I do. You're talking about Pasta Perfect."

"I am. Have you been there yet?"

"No, but all the other teachers rave about it."

"Then you should see if it's worth all the great reviews."

"It would have to be just dinner. And I can't say yes for sure until I talk to Hayley."

"Then say maybe and let me know."

She let out a breath. "You're very persistent. Why?"

"I don't think a woman has ever asked me why before."

"Well, I'm asking. Why do you want to take me out?"

"Because I haven't been able to stop thinking about you."

Her cheeks flushed and her dark eyes brightened at his words, making her even prettier. She had no idea how beautiful she was, how appealing, how desirable. She couldn't get away from being a mom, but he saw the woman she was, not just her role as Brandon's mother.

"It's hard to say no to that," she murmured.

He gave her a slow smile as their gazes met. "You asked me why; I answered. Now why don't you give me your number, and I'll give you mine, and we'll touch base tomorrow after you check with your babysitter?"

"Okay," she said, taking out her phone so they could exchange numbers.

They'd just finished doing that when a silver Toyota Scion came squealing into the parking lot. His heart quickened.

"Who's that?" Jessica asked.

"My sister," he replied, as Tara jumped out of the car. Dressed in skinny jeans and a knit top, her brown hair pulled back in a ponytail, she looked young. She also looked pissed off, her green eyes spitting fire.

"What the hell is she thinking?" Tara demanded when she got within ten feet of him. "Do you know what she's doing now?"

His gut clenched. "Are you talking about Mom?"

"What other crazy person would I be talking about?" Tara retorted. "She just texted me. She's getting married. Yes, that's right. She's going to marry the yoga guy who took her to India. It's happening in two weeks in India. She's not even coming back here. And then she's going to go on a honeymoon—to Morocco, of all places."

"That's ridiculous." As he finished speaking, his phone buzzed—a message from his mother.

"That's her, isn't it?" Tara asked.

"Look, I should go," Jessica interrupted. "I'll

leave you to this."

"Wait," he said. "Jessica, this is my sister, Tara."

"Hi, Tara," Jessica said somewhat awkwardly.

"Hi," Tara muttered, barely giving her a look.

"I'll talk to you tomorrow," he told Jessica. "Make a plan for our evening."

"Maybe you need to deal with this."

"Trust me, I'll be dealing with this before then." He moved Tara away from the car as Jessica got into her vehicle and pulled out of the lot. Then he read the message on his phone.

"Well?" Tara demanded. "Did she tell you anything different?"

"No, just what she told you. I'll call her." He punched in his mother's number and let it ring.

"She won't answer."

"She has to be awake; she just texted me."

"And she knows if she speaks to you that you'll try to talk her out of it."

His mother's phone went to voicemail. He didn't leave a message. Instead, he texted her back: *We need to talk. Tara is upset and so am I. You owe us a call. We're together now, so call me back.*

Tara paced around the lot. "I can't believe it. How can she do this, Reid? How can she marry someone I've never even met? I'm her daughter. And I'm not even going to be there for her wedding."

He looked into his sister's eyes and saw not just anger but also pain. "She's impulsive, you know that. She's not thinking."

"What if she doesn't come back at all?" Tara asked, fear replacing the anger and pain. "It's my senior year. What am I supposed to do? Live by myself? Stay with my friends? Move in with you?"

None of those options sounded good to him, but Tara wasn't really looking for an answer from him. She needed to vent, so he let her.

"How can she just leave me? The winter formal is in two weeks. I wanted her to go dress shopping with me and take pictures and do what the other moms do." Her bottom lip trembled and her eyes blurred with tears, and suddenly she wasn't seventeen anymore—she was five, and he was the big brother who wanted to take care of her.

He threw his arms around her and gave her a hug. "It's going to be okay. We'll talk to her. She'll come back."

"With him? With this man I don't even know?"

He wished he could say no, but how could he? His mother did what she wanted most of the time. Maybe he could find a way to talk her into waiting until Tara left for college.

Tara pulled away from him with a sniff. "I don't matter to her at all."

"You do matter. She loves you. She just doesn't always think before she acts. She gets caught up in her quests, and she forgets that there are real-life responsibilities to take care of. Speaking of which, do I need to step in on bills? Do you need money?"

"She paid a bunch of stuff before she left, and she gave me some cash."

"All right. Well, you tell me if you need more or anything else." He glanced down at his phone again, but there was no answering text. His mother hated conflict, especially with her kids. "Why don't you come inside? Mason is making chili, and it's always good."

She shook her head. "I look ugly now," she said,

wiping her eyes.

"No, you don't."

"Well, Melanie and I are going to study for a test tomorrow."

"Okay. I will get a hold of Mom. I promise."

"It probably won't matter. I texted her, too. She didn't answer." She drew in a deep breath and let it out. "Sorry I'm being a baby. I just couldn't believe it."

"I understand. It's shocking. I remember when she told me she was getting married on a getaway weekend to Vegas. You were seven and I was nineteen."

"She made you come home to watch me. I remember that."

"Well, I wanted to be there for you."

"You took me to the pumpkin festival, and I rode the ponies and we ate pumpkin pie and pumpkin cookies and pumpkin ice cream."

"And then you got sick," he said with a laugh.

"Yeah," she said, grinning back at him. "I've never eaten pumpkin anything again."

"Jerry was a nice enough guy."

"He was, but I knew him before they got married. This new guy I haven't even met. I probably shouldn't worry. Jerry lasted five years. This guy probably won't even last that long."

"You might be right." He was happy to see that she was calmer now. "Whatever happens, we'll deal with it together. You're not alone in this, Tara."

"Thanks, Reid. So, who was that woman you were talking to?"

"That was Jessica."

"She's pretty. Are you dating her?"

"I'm trying," he said with a smile.

Tara gave him a doubtful look. "Trying? No woman says no to you."

He laughed. "Some women do. Now, are you sure I can't talk you into some chili?"

"No, I'm going to eat at Melanie's."

"Okay, drive more slowly on the way there. I don't care how pissed off you are. You need to be responsible behind the wheel."

She rolled her eyes. "I'm a very good driver, Reid."

"Let's keep it that way. Call me if you hear from Mom."

"You do the same, but I'm not holding my breath. The next time she gets in touch, she'll probably already be married."

He had a feeling Tara might be right. His family drama never seemed to end. Every time he thought it was coming to a close, something else happened. He hated that his mother was putting his sister through this. *Six more months,* he told himself. *Then Tara would move on with her life, and he could move on with his.*

She was tempting fate, Jessica thought, as she slid into the chair across from Reid at Pasta Perfect on Tuesday night. She'd had twenty-four hours to find a way out of their date, but she hadn't come up with anything, so against her better judgment, here she was.

She told herself it was just one date, and then that would be it. She also told herself that she was paying Reid back for being so nice to Brandon, but that wasn't really the reason she was here.

She'd wanted to see Reid again. She'd wanted the chance to spend more time with him. And now she had that time. But her heart was beating a million miles a minute, her palms were sweating, and there were butterflies in her stomach.

Reid didn't look nervous at all. He just looked mouth-wateringly attractive. His hair was styled back, his face cleanly shaven, his blue eyes sparkling with humor and mischief. He was a troublemaker, no doubt about it. He was also a happy person, and she liked being around that. Kevin had been more of a moody guy; she'd always had to tread on eggshells around him, not sure what he was thinking or how he would react to something.

Reid seemed like a much more direct person. He asked for what he wanted, and he stated his intentions. Those intentions made her wary, but they also made her pulse pound in a way that it hadn't in a long time.

As the waitress came over to take their drink order, she took a glance at the cocktail menu but decided to stick with a glass of red wine. Reid did the same and told the waitress they would need a few more minutes to decide on dinner.

"What's good here?" she asked.

"Everything. I've had most of the pastas. The minestrone soup is also excellent, and the bread is magnificent," he added, as the busboy set down a basket of warm focaccia bread and a plate of oil and vinegar.

She couldn't resist snatching a piece of that warm bread and popping it into her mouth. "It tastes amazing."

"I'm glad you like it. I'm also glad you came."

"Me, too. Hopefully, we'll both feel the same way at the end of the evening."

He smiled. "That would be the hope."

"So what happened with your mom and your sister?"

He sighed as he set down his menu. "It's a messy drama. My mom decided to get married to a man my sister and I have never met. She wouldn't answer either of our texts or phone calls until this afternoon. She says she's in love with her yoga instructor, who took her to India for a retreat. In between meditation, romantic walks, and spicy hot curry, she decided to marry him."

"How long has she known him?"

"About two months."

"That's fast."

"It's ridiculous. I told her that the least she could do was wait until after Tara graduates. Then she can marry him. But to do it now, in India, without her family, without us even meeting the guy—it's wrong."

"It's hurtful," she said, seeing pain in his eyes.

"I don't care, but I do feel bad for my sister. She's afraid my mother isn't going to come back, that she's going to be fending for herself the next few months. She's got the winter formal coming up in two weeks and apparently is worried about getting a dress. Then there are awards for senior year, and a lot of big graduation events."

"Is your mom going through with the marriage?"

"She said she'd think about it. But we'll see. I honestly wouldn't put it past her to marry him over there and come back and move him into the house."

"Has she been with other men since your father?"

"Yes. She married one of them in Vegas. He

lasted a few years. Another guy, she moved into the house for a while. He was actually decent, but my mother got bored with him and out he went. There hasn't been anyone the last two years and I think Tara was enjoying having our mother to herself, but that's over."

She gave him a sympathetic smile. "It's too bad we don't get to pick our parents."

"Isn't that the truth. How do you get along with your parents? I know you said they weren't happy with you when you got pregnant. But that's changed, right?"

"Marginally. My mom was recently diagnosed with an early stage of breast cancer. Her prognosis is good, but I think the health scare has mellowed her out a little. She hasn't been as critical of me in recent months as she used to be."

"I can't imagine what she could criticize about you."

"Oh, everything. My hair, my nails, the clothes I wear, the fact that I teach elementary school and not college, which would be much more impressive in their eyes. Trust me, it's a long list."

"She's crazy."

"My father is even worse. I will say one thing, though. My father's harsh and high standards always made me try harder. I just never quite got to the top, at least in his mind. My brother is really the apple of both of their eyes. Mine, too. Christopher is a good guy, and he's going to be a terrific doctor."

"Well, you're not doing badly yourself. Teaching kids is one of the most noble jobs there is. You're molding the next generation."

"Sometimes it's hard to remember that when I'm

picking glue out of my hair." She gave him a dimpled smile. "I would say thanks, but I know you hate the word."

He laughed. "We're getting to know each other well."

"Right now, I need to get to know this menu a little better."

For the next few minutes, they perused the list of entrees and then placed their orders. She opted for the linguine with clams while Reid selected the scallops and risotto.

"How was your lunch with your friends?" he asked her, as the waitress took their menus.

"It was fun. Everyone except one person made it. I found out one of them just got engaged and two of them announced they are pregnant, so along with bridal showers, there will be baby showers coming up, too." She paused. "It was good to see them. There aren't that many people in my life who have been there for me through everything, but they have, and they never judged me. I'm lucky that I have such good girlfriends."

"Friends are important," he agreed. "By the way, I called the Ritz and set up a birthday spa day for Tara and three friends next week. That's going to set me back some cash, but I think she needs a special day even more now. I told her about it this afternoon, and she actually said she was impressed with my gift. It's been awhile since I've impressed her in any way, so thank you for that."

"You can thank me, but I can't thank you?" she teased.

He tipped his head. "Good point. But that's only the first time for me."

"Are you implying I haven't been as generous as you?"

He laughed. "Walked right into that one, didn't I?"

She liked how easy it was to be with Reid. He made her laugh. He made her feel like life wasn't as serious as she sometimes made it. "You did."

"You have a great smile, Jess. You should use it more often. It's like the sun coming out from behind the clouds."

That was actually a great description for how she felt when she was with him, and it was that feeling that made the cautious voice inside her head scream *danger zone*.

"Life isn't always sunny. There isn't always something to smile about," she said.

"Ah, there it goes again—behind the clouds."

"You can be annoying," she said.

He gave her an easy nod. "I know. I don't always think before I speak. You're obviously sensitive about your smile."

"I am not sensitive about my smile," she argued, then found herself smiling again when she saw the teasing gleam in his eyes. "Let's talk about something else."

"Good idea. You asked me why I wanted to take you out, and I told you. So, now it's my turn to ask—why did you say yes?"

She thought for a moment and decided to be honest. "Because I couldn't say no."

His eyes darkened. "Yeah?"

"Yeah," she murmured, meeting his gaze. "But I've been telling myself that it's only going to be one date."

"So I have my work cut out for me. Okay, I'm up for the challenge."

"It wasn't a challenge; it was a fact."

"We'll see if I can change your mind."

She realized that she'd just played her hand all wrong, but it was too late to take it back. "I can be stubborn," she told him.

"So can I," he returned with a sexy grin that told her keeping him to one date was going to be a challenge for her too.

Eight

Over dinner, their conversation turned to less personal topics as Reid shared stories about growing up in Half Moon Bay and life in the firehouse, and she filled him in on some of the funnier things her first-graders had said to her. By the time they finished up a decadent and rich chocolate dessert, she was feeling relaxed and mellow and almost a little sad that the time had gone by so fast.

Reid was a good talker—never shy on having something to say—but he was also a good listener, and they seemed to share a lot of similar opinions about the world, probably because they both served the public and had a sense of responsibility to the community that she didn't always find in others. Reid might be a surfer and a charming daredevil, but he also risked his life every day, and while he downplayed the risk, she knew it couldn't be easy doing what he did. It wasn't easy doing what she did, either. Kids could be challenging in a lot of ways, and their parents even more so.

"So tell me what you like to do when you're not

teaching and being a mom," Reid said, interrupting her thoughts.

She wiped her mouth with a napkin and then set it down on the table. "There isn't much extra time, but I do like to draw."

"Really? What do you draw?"

"All kinds of things, but mostly illustrations. I like to draw children and superheroes and figures that might appear in a kid's book. It's just a hobby, but I have thought about one day turning my illustrations into a book. In fact, Brandon helps me write the stories. We have a couple of books that we've sort of loosely put together."

"That's cool. I'd like to see them sometime."

"They need a lot of work. I'm sure they're not that good."

"Are you being modest or telling the truth?" he challenged.

She hesitated, then shrugged. "Okay, they're pretty good."

He gave her a grin of approval. "Nothing wrong with being proud of your work. How long have you been drawing?"

"Since I was Brandon's age. I was always doodling and coloring in my spare time. I'd make up stories in my head and then bring them to life on scraps of paper. My parents did not like that at all. They both thought I should be spending more time on my math and science homework. I did what was expected but never anything more. I just didn't like numbers. It was always art for me. I love creating something from nothing, bringing words to life. I'm a very visual person, so art is meaningful to me." She paused. "And, wow, that was a little over-the-top reply to your very simple question."

"Hey, don't stop talking. I like hearing the passion in your voice. It's good to do something you love."

"I do love being a teacher," she stressed. "And I do love teaching math and science to my kids. They weren't my best subjects, but they are very important, especially in our technologically driven world."

"I agree, but I'm betting art has a big place in your classroom as well."

"It does. Art is so good for the kids. They can express themselves in ways they can't with words or logic. They're young. Their minds are open to every possibility, and in art there are no limitations."

"You don't make them color within the lines, do you?"

"Definitely not," she said with a laugh. "Some kids prefer that option, though. I've had children tell me they want to color inside something, not just face a blank page. So I offer a mix of both. Some kids like structure, some don't."

"Well, I wasn't big on coloring," he confessed. "But Tara loved nothing more than coloring books when she was little. And she definitely liked the lines. Sometimes she'd make me color with her, and she would get so mad and so bossy when I went outside the line."

"I'm not a psychologist, but I do know a lot about children, and I'm betting, from what I've heard of your family life, that Tara found comfort in drawing inside a world of structure, one where there were rules, and you knew what you had to do to make something pretty."

Reid stared back at her, a more serious gleam in his eyes. "That makes a lot of sense. But why didn't I feel that way? I grew up like she did."

"Because you're different. You probably wanted to find a whole new world so coloring over the lines was freeing. It's the same with surfing. It offered an escape, didn't it? The challenge of riding the waves and winning probably also gave you a sense of control. If you could beat the ocean, you could beat anything." She licked her lips. "But like I said, I'm not a psychologist, so my opinion could be worth absolutely nothing."

"No, I like your opinions. You're very intuitive. Do you have that same keen insight about yourself?"

"Definitely not," she said with a laugh.

He smiled back. "Sometimes we need an outside opinion."

"So, what do you like to do when you're not on the ocean or in the firehouse?" she asked. "Any other hobbies?"

"Mostly sports. I play softball in the summer and basketball in the winter. I've been getting into biking lately. There's a good ocean trail that runs about six miles. I sometimes take my bike out there."

"I'll have to check that trail out. Is it only for serious bikers? Or could a mom and her kid use it?"

"It's for everyone. It's wide and pretty flat, although the last mile or two go uphill."

"Well, I don't think Brandon could make it six miles, but he does love to ride his bike."

"Another good place for kids to ride is Miramonte Park. It has a great bike path through some very tall trees. I used to take Tara out there to ride. She really liked it."

"You're very close to your sister, aren't you?"

"I try to keep an eye on her. When she was a little

kid, I was her hero. But when she hit her teens, I became her annoying big brother with few heroic traits."

"I don't know about that. She came running to you yesterday, looking for that hero."

"She was overwhelmed by anxiety. I hope my mother reconsiders this marriage idea and that she comes back and takes care of her daughter for the next few months, but I'm not sure that will happen. If it doesn't, Tara will have to deal with the disappointment."

"And you'll help her with that."

"I will try, but I don't know if it will be enough. I can't replace her mom."

His words resonated deep within her. "You know, I say that to myself all the time. I worry that I'm not enough for Brandon, because no matter how hard I try, I can't be his dad. But you know, it's not about the quantity of people in your life; it's the quality. I had both my parents. I'm not close to them at all and had very little support from either one of them."

"What about your brother? Are you close to him?"

She smiled. "Yes. Christopher is a pain in the ass, but I love him, and we were close growing up. He was the bridge between me and my parents. He had the uncanny ability to always make my parents laugh, which usually took the heat off one or both of us. Fortunately, he didn't just use his superpower for himself."

"You said he's studying to be a doctor. Is he local?"

"No, he's back east—Harvard Medical School, my father's alma mater."

"Top of the line."

"He's very smart."

"What kind of doctor does he want to be?"

"A neurosurgeon."

"Is that what your dad is?"

"No. My father is a surgeon, but he specializes in orthopedics. He's quite well-known in his field. He's written a lot of papers, and he teaches at medical schools around the country. He's very well-respected."

"Does he or your mom spend much time with Brandon?"

"Not in the past, but I'm hoping since we're closer now that they'll have a better relationship. Brandon would love to get to know them. He has no contact whatsoever with Kevin's parents, so it would be nice if he could get to know my parents better. But while my mom is undergoing treatment, she's a little reluctant to be around small children germs. Once she's free and clear, that should change." She let out a sigh. "I should probably call it a night. It's a school night—for both me and Brandon."

He laughed. "It's been a long time since a date said that to me."

"Probably not since you were in high school."

"Probably."

"Have you ever gone out with a woman who had a child before?"

"Nope. You're the first."

"It's different."

"Different doesn't scare me."

"Nothing scares you," she said. "I get it."

"I didn't say *nothing*, but dating a woman with a child doesn't even make the list."

"It's not just different; it's complicated. I can't just

think about myself. I have to protect Brandon."

"I wouldn't hurt Brandon," he said, a serious note in his voice. "I would never do that."

"You might not mean to, but just having him start thinking of you as someone who might be in his life for a while could end up in disappointment, and I really don't want that to happen. That's why I decided that tonight has to be our first and last date."

"You didn't have fun?"

"Of course I did. I had a lot of fun."

"Then change your mind. Give me a second date."

"It's not you, Reid; it's just the situation. If I were single…"

"You are single."

"Divorced and a mother."

"But still deserving a life for yourself, Jess."

"I know that," she said. "And I'm not against a relationship, but it would have to go really, really slow, and I'd want assurances and promises and all kinds of things you wouldn't want to make."

"How do you know that?"

"What's your longest relationship to date?" she asked.

"I don't know—several months, close to a year."

"So you're thirty years old, and you've never gone out with someone for more than several months. You just made my point."

He frowned. "Maybe there was no one worth going out with for longer than that. You didn't meet any of them."

"I don't want to argue with you, Reid. You're a great guy. You could have anyone."

"Apparently not," he said dryly. "I'll take you

home now. But I'm not giving up on that second date. Just so you know."

She didn't argue. She'd said what had to be said, and eventually Reid would accept it.

That thought made her feel a little depressed, though. It was fun and flattering to be pursued by an attractive man and Reid had made her feel young and wanted. It was hard to say no to that. Part of her was tempted to see where things could go, but she wouldn't just be risking her heart. At the end of the day, she still had a seven-year-old waiting for her at home, and as she'd just told Reid, Brandon had to come first.

Jessica was pushing him away as hard and as fast as she could, but despite the words that had come out of her mouth, Reid had seen a different story in her eyes. He'd seen yearning and desire and that's why he wasn't going to back off.

If she wasn't interested, he'd know it, and he'd let her go. But until then...

Until then what?

The question ran around in his head as he drove her home and walked her to her door. She'd made it clear she was done after tonight. *How was he going to get around that?*

"Well, goodnight," Jessica said, pausing before putting her key into the door.

"I just want to make sure you get all the way in," he said, buying a few more seconds.

"Fine." She opened the door and walked into the entry.

A teenaged girl came down the hall. "You're back early."

"Hi, Hayley. How did it go?" Jessica asked.

"Great. Brandon did all his homework. He's super easy to watch."

"I'm glad to hear that." Jessica pulled out her wallet and took out some cash. "Here you go. Thanks again."

"Any time." Hayley gave Reid a somewhat assessing look, then glanced back at Jessica. "Did you have fun?"

"We did. We went to Pasta Perfect. It was very good."

"My family loves that place," Hayley said.

"Thanks again."

"No problem." Hayley slipped on her jacket and headed out of the house.

"Nice that you don't have to drive her home," he commented.

"Yes, it's very convenient." She pulled out her phone as it began to ring, her brows drawing together. "It's my father. He never calls me."

"Take it."

She answered the phone. "Hello? Dad? Is something wrong?"

As Jessica moved into the living room to speak to her father, Brandon came down the stairs in his pajamas, a sleepy look in his brown eyes, but he got more alert when he saw Reid, giving a happy and surprised smile.

"Hi, Reid," he said.

"Hey, Brandon. Did you have fun tonight?"

Brandon nodded. "Where's Mom?"

"She's talking to your grandfather." As he

finished speaking, Jessica came back into the room, her face pale. Whatever her father had had to say hadn't been good.

"Brandon," Jessica said. "Are you ready for bed?"

He nodded. "Can you read to me?"

"I'll be up in a minute. Why don't you go upstairs and pick out a book?"

"Okay. Good-night, Reid," Brandon said, as he ran up the stairs.

"Sleep well," he said, thinking Brandon was a lot easier than Tara when it came to going to bed. At that age, his sister used to fight like crazy for even an extra minute past her bedtime. When Brandon had disappeared up the stairs, he glanced at Jessica. "What's wrong?"

"My mom is in the hospital. She felt dizzy, so her friend took her to the emergency room. My dad's plane is delayed. He's been in LA the last few days. He wants me to go to the hospital and check on Mom. But I have Brandon. I can't ask Hayley to stay late into the night. Maybe her mom could do it, but I don't really know her that well yet."

"I can stay here and watch Brandon while you're gone," he suggested.

She hesitated. "I can't ask you to do that, Reid."

"I offered. I'm here. I'm willing. Let me help."

"Are you sure? I know it's a huge favor to ask."

"Jessica, it's not a big deal. I'll stay here as long as you need me to. I don't work tomorrow, so I can get Brandon to school if you need me to."

"I'll be back tonight, but it might be late."

"Don't worry about it."

"Okay. I'll tell Brandon I have to go see my mom but I won't mention anything about the hospital."

"Sounds like a plan," he said following her up the stairs.

Jessica walked over to the bed where Brandon had surrounded himself with a pile of books. "I have to go out for a while to see Grandma," she said. "Reid is going to stay with you until I get back."

"Why do you have to go there now?" Brandon asked with annoyance. "You just got home."

"I know, but Grandma needs my help," she replied.

"I could go with you."

"It's past your bedtime. You have school tomorrow."

Brandon's eyes grew stubborn. "I can stay up late. I'm not tired. I want to go with you."

"Well, you can't," she said a weary note in her voice.

Reid saw the storm clouds gathering in Brandon's eyes. "You know," he interrupted, "I'm not tired, either. What do you say we read one of your favorite books, Brandon?"

Brandon debated his offer for a minute. "Can we read two books?"

He laughed. "You're going to be a good negotiator."

"What does that mean?" Brandon asked, wide-eyed.

"It means, yes, I will read two books with you, if it's okay with your mom."

Jessica nodded. "But that's all. Then you go to sleep, Brandon. No pushing Reid to do one more."

"Okay."

"I love you," Jessica said, giving Brandon a hug and a kiss.

Reid felt a rush of unexpected emotion watching Jessica and her son. There was a lot of love between them. Brandon had no idea how lucky he was.

"Thanks again," Jessica said, giving him a grateful smile as she moved toward the door.

"Drive safe."

"I will. I'll be back as soon as I can."

"We'll be fine. Don't worry."

As Jessica left the room, Reid moved around the bed and sat down next to Brandon, who handed him a three-ring binder.

"What's this? I thought we were going to read some books."

"It's Mommy's book," Brandon said. "She drew the pictures, and I helped her write it."

"Okay."

He opened the binder and saw a colorful illustration of a little boy about Brandon's age who was carrying a backpack and walking along a garden path with a leprechaun peeking out from behind a rock. The lines were precise. The characters felt very real, and the colors were amazing. "Your mom drew this?"

Brandon nodded. "Yes. I wanted to read a story about a leprechaun, so she made one for me. It's about a little boy who needs to catch a leprechaun so he can get three wishes. So he goes to Ireland to find one. Have you ever been to Ireland?"

"I have not, but I'm curious to see what happens in this book."

Reid turned the pages as Brandon basically read the story to him. It was clear that Brandon had it memorized.

Reid wasn't as much caught up in the words as he

was in the pictures. Jessica was clearly talented. And it was a shame that this story was just in a three-ring binder by Brandon's bed. It should be published and be in schools and libraries. He wondered if she had those kinds of plans for it.

He suspected she didn't want to think that big, didn't want to do anything that might infringe on her time with Brandon, her job as a mom. She was trying to be a superwoman: a mom, a dad, a teacher, and now a good daughter. He doubted being an illustrator was too high on the list, but maybe it should be.

He wished he could take some of the burden off her shoulders. He wanted to do more than just babysit her kid, and it was a rather shocking feeling.

He'd spent half his life taking care of his sister and his mother, and it was almost time for him to be completely free of those entanglements. Why would he want to take on more responsibilities now?

And it wasn't like Jessica wanted him to volunteer. She was doing everything to push him away.

Maybe he should listen to her.

He liked her. He was attracted to her. He wanted to spend more time with her, but was he really looking for this kind of life? Did he want to be in a relationship with a woman who had a child? Did he want nights of story time and needing to find babysitters so they could be alone? He'd never had to deal with any of that in his social life. But then he'd never met anyone like Jessica before.

He tried not to think about it. He didn't like putting too much worry into the future. He'd learned a long time ago that he couldn't necessarily stop what was coming, so he should just live in the moment and deal with problems when they actually occurred.

Jessica was the opposite. She spent a lot of time trying to avoid potential problems. Which was why she'd said no more dates.

Was he just being obstinate? Competitive? Trying to change her mind to see if he could?

No, it was more than that. Because if he wasn't really interested, he would back off. Brandon was important to him, too.

He suddenly realized that Brandon was no longer talking. He'd fallen asleep.

He slipped quietly out of the bed, put the books on the desk and then tucked the covers around Brandon's small body.

"Reid," Brandon muttered.

"Yes?" he asked.

Brandon gave him a sleepy look. "Will you come back another time and read to me?"

"Sure," he said.

He didn't know if Brandon had heard him, because his eyes were closed again, but he did know he would keep the promise no matter what Jessica said. She didn't want to disappoint her son; he didn't, either. Beyond that, who knew?

Nine

"I want to go home. I don't need to be here," her mom said, waving her hand around the hospital room. "I feel fine now. It was just a dizzy spell. Tell the doctor I want to leave."

Even in a hospital gown, her mother was a force to be reckoned with. She'd always had a demanding personality, which was why she pretty much ran every group she was in, from the PTA to the country club and the library board. But Jessica couldn't let her mother's dislike of hospitals prevent her from getting the best possible care.

"They want you to stay until the morning just to be sure," she replied.

"Well, I don't want to stay. So tell them to release me."

"It's only for a few hours. You'll go to sleep. In the morning, Dad will take you home. Is it really that bad?"

"Yes, it is. I'm not sick."

"Why do you think you fainted?"

"Because I stood up too fast and Gwen gets

hysterical at the least little thing," she said, referring to her longtime friend. "She insisted on bringing me here, and as soon as those doctors found out I was on chemo, they made me go through all kinds of uncomfortable tests. And where is your father?"

"I told you, his plane was delayed. He'll be here as soon as he gets back. I'm sure he won't even go home first."

"He better not. I don't like this, Jessica."

For the first time, she heard a note of fear in her mother's voice, and she impulsively put a hand on her mom's arm. She couldn't remember the last time they'd touched. She was also shocked at how thin her mom had become. "It's going to be okay," she said. "This is just a little setback. It's not something to worry about."

Her mom stared back at her with eyes that were the same color as her own. "You were always a terrible liar, Jessica. Your brother was much better than you were."

"Well, Christopher was better than me at most everything," she said dryly.

"Where is Brandon?"

"He's at home. I left him with a babysitter," she said, thinking that Reid was definitely not the typical babysitter, but tonight he was a lifesaver.

"You should go home and be with him."

"I'll leave when Dad gets here. I don't want you to be alone."

"Well," her mom said, as if surprised by the sentiment. "All right then."

She was happy that the immediate battle appeared to be over. "Is there anything I can get you? Are you cold? Do you need more blankets? Another pillow?"

"No, nothing will make this room or this bed comfortable. How is Brandon liking Half Moon Bay?"

"He's happy that there's a beach nearby."

"Have you taken him to the tide pools?"

"Several times. He loves them. He's an explorer at heart."

"You used to like going there, too."

She was surprised her mom remembered that. Actually, she was surprised her mother knew that. She'd always gone to the tide pools with a nanny or someone else's mom.

"You'd come back with wet shoes and sandy socks," her mom continued. "And you never remembered to leave them in the mud room."

She sighed, thinking that the happy memory was not so happy anymore.

"Is Brandon making friends?" her mom asked.

She thought it was interesting that her mom couldn't ask her if she was happy or making friends; it was all about Brandon—the grandson she barely knew. "He is," she said, knowing this wasn't the time to get into any kind of argument.

The door opened and her father entered the room. A tall man with silver hair and dark-brown eyes, her father had always had an imposing presence. Without saying a word, he demanded attention and respect. She suspected the medical students he worked with cowered when he came near, or maybe that was just her.

But she really shouldn't cower anymore. She was a grown woman with her own child, her own life.

"Thank goodness you're here," her mom said, as her father rushed across the room to take her mother's hand.

"What happened?" he asked.

"I just felt dizzy and Gwen overreacted, rushing me here to the hospital, when all I did was stand up too fast."

Her father picked up her chart and read through the medical notes. "It doesn't look like they found anything unusual during your exam."

"Nothing more unusual than the fact that I've had chemo and dizziness can be a side effect," her mother said shortly. "I want to go home."

"I don't see any reason why you shouldn't. I'll talk to the nurses."

"Thank you," her mother said. "I told Jessica to go talk to them, but she didn't feel comfortable asking them to release me."

"Well, I'm here," he said. "I'll talk to them."

As her father left, she turned back to her mom. "You know it wasn't that I didn't feel comfortable asking the nurses a question; I just thought it best you follow doctor's orders."

"Your father's a doctor. He'll take care of me."

"I know he will." She let out a breath. "I'm glad you're feeling better. I know the treatment is hard on you."

"I just want it to be over. I want to feel normal again. I want to play tennis and bridge with my friends. I want to think about planning our vacation, not scheduling a doctor's appointment."

"It will be over soon." They'd caught her mother's cancer in the earliest stage, so hopefully she would be completely fine. She just hoped this recent dizzy spell wasn't a sign of something else.

Her father re-entered the room. "You can go home."

"Thank goodness," her mother said with relief.

"You can go home, too," he told Jessica. "Thank you for coming."

"You're welcome. I'll check in with you tomorrow, Mom."

Her parents muttered good-night, as they focused on getting her mom dressed and ready to leave.

As she walked out to her car, she thought about how close her parents were. They might be distant from her, but there had always been a strong, loving bond between them. Sometimes they felt like an island unto themselves.

She knew they loved her in their own way, and she loved them. They were her parents. They'd taken care of her as best as they could. She just didn't feel close to them—not the way she felt close to Brandon. He was her whole life.

Would that be different if she had a husband?

She didn't think so. She had enough love for a man and a child or any number of children.

But her parents almost seemed like they'd had kids just because it was expected, not because her mom had really wanted to be a mother.

While she hadn't exactly made the choice to have a child, she loved Brandon desperately, and she was invested in him. She took pleasure in watching him do whatever he was doing: sports, art, music. She loved talking to him, seeing his brain in action when he figured out a problem.

But maybe her parents' lack of interest in her life was partly why she wanted to be there for Brandon. She never wanted him to feel like an outsider, which was why she'd always been careful about bringing anyone else into her life.

As she started her drive back to Half Moon Bay, her thoughts drifted to Reid. Considering his generous offer to babysit tonight, she had a feeling she owed him at least one more date. She smiled at that thought. It wouldn't be a hardship to go out with him again. She liked him a lot. Tonight she'd gotten to know him a little better, and it had only teased her desire to know more.

It was dangerous to go down that road. Every instinct she had told her it probably wouldn't end well, that their lives were too different, but she wanted to see around the next bend. She told herself she could stop things any time she wanted. It didn't have to end in disaster; it could just end. *Couldn't it?*

Reid was sitting on the couch in the family room, watching the news when she entered the adjoining kitchen. He got to his feet when she walked in, concern in his blue eyes.

"Everything okay?" he asked.

"Yes. How was Brandon?"

"Perfect. He fell asleep about a half hour after you left. How's your mom?"

"Okay." She dropped her bag on the counter and walked over to the couch. They sat down together. "She had a dizzy spell, but they didn't find anything wrong with her. It was probably just a side effect from the chemo she's been having."

"I'm glad she's all right."

"She had enough energy to be mad as hell that she was in the hospital, so that's probably a good sign. My dad came and he got them to release her, so he's in charge now." She glanced down at the coffee table, startled to see three of her story binders there. "What are these doing down here?"

"I took them from Brandon's room after he fell asleep. We read the first one together. I wanted to see what the others were about. Your work is amazing, by the way."

"The stories are kind of silly, but Brandon and I have fun together making them up."

"The stories are good, but the art brings them to life. You were being too modest earlier, Jessica. You're incredibly talented. You should publish those books."

"I don't know if that's easy to do, but I might look into it—someday."

"What's stopping you from doing it now?" he challenged.

"I'm busy. I have a lot on my plate."

"Is it really a time issue, or are you afraid to find out if they're good enough?"

"You ask a lot of hard questions."

"Not that hard. You already know the answer."

"Fine. I might be a little afraid to find out just how good they are. It's easier to keep them as a hobby."

"That's fair. But I think you should take a chance. Your talent is too good not to share."

She was touched by his encouragement. She hadn't had a lot of cheerleaders in her life, but for some reason, Reid appeared to be one.

"We should do some research into publishing companies," Reid continued. "One of my friends runs a bookstore downtown. She might know someone."

"I've been in that store. They have a great

children's section."

"I'll introduce you to Kelly when you're ready. I'm sure she has some contacts or knows something about publishing."

"Okay, but slow down. I will look into it, but I'm still getting settled here, and I just need my life to calm down a little."

"All right, I'll stop pushing."

"Really? Because that doesn't seem likely," she said dryly.

He laughed. "Sorry, but I can't help it. When I see someone wasting their talent, I have to say something."

"Maybe I should watch you surf one day and see if you're wasting your talent."

"Any time. You're more than welcome."

"I really appreciate you covering for me tonight," she told him. "Seriously, it would have been difficult for me to find anyone else, and I couldn't really take him to the hospital."

"It really wasn't a big deal. Brandon talked non-stop for thirty minutes, then crashed. He fell asleep so fast, I thought he might be faking it."

She nodded. "He does that all the time. He fights going to sleep and then his body just says enough is enough and he's off to dreamland in a split second. I wish I could fall asleep that easily. What about you? Can you drop off like that?"

"I have trained myself to find sleep as quickly as possible. At the firehouse, you never know how many hours you're going to get, so I take what I can get."

"It must be really weird to be woken up in the middle of the night to go put out a fire. Does that happen a lot?"

"This isn't the busiest or biggest city so we don't get as many calls as an urban firehouse would get, but a fair amount. It's not just fires but also accidents, both home and vehicular, along with the occasional woman stuck in a doghouse."

She made a face at him. "Let's not talk about that."

"I'm grateful to Wiley. He made our first meeting memorable."

"Speaking of which…let me guess Wiley is sleeping on Brandon's bed."

"He is. I wasn't sure if that was allowed, but he seemed fairly determined and I didn't want to wake up Brandon."

"It's fine. I let him sleep there. It actually keeps Brandon in his bed. When he wakes up, he just cuddles up with Wiley."

"I would have loved to have a dog when I was Brandon's age."

"Your mother wouldn't let you?" she asked curiously.

"No, we had a cat for a while, but it ran away and never came back. That was kind of what happened in my house. What about you? Did you have a pet?"

"No, my mom refused, and my dad went along with whatever she wanted. She liked her house clean and free of pet hair, as well as kid's toys. We had a housecleaning service that came in once a week, and my nanny was usually expected to do some cleaning along with childcare."

"You had a nanny?"

"Several. They were nice, mostly young women, although there was one old, stern-faced woman I couldn't stand. Fortunately, she left after a few months."

"Did your mom work? Is that why you had a nanny?"

"She didn't work for money, but she volunteered for a lot of organizations. She liked to be in charge. Most people thought she was super generous and benevolent, but I always kind of thought she was more in it for the power and all the gratitude that people gave her. She really fed off that. And of course she was a devoted wife. My parents are very close. They might not get along with me, but they get along great with each other." She paused. "And I am probably boring you to sleep. I'm surprised you haven't nodded off yet."

"Not a chance. I find you fascinating, Jessica."

"Well, this fascinating woman should probably say good-night. It's almost midnight and mornings come early around here." She got to her feet. "I'll walk you to the door."

Reid followed her down the hall. She opened the door, shivering as the night air blew in. But she liked the chill; there was always a little too much heat when Reid was around.

"So, Jess," he said, moving in a little too close.

Her heart sped up at the purposeful look in his eyes. "Yes?"

"Don't you think I've earned a second date?"

She'd thought he was going to kiss her, so it took her a second to reply to his question. "I guess I really can't say no, can I?"

He took her hands in his. "Only if you honestly don't want to go out with me," he said. "If that's the truth, then tell me to my face."

She stared at his handsome face and knew those

words couldn't possibly pass through her lips. "I honestly can't say that, Reid. But all the reasons I gave you before still stand."

"We'll talk about those on our next date. What are you doing tomorrow?"

"Tomorrow is the winter concert at Brandon's school. I can't miss it. Brandon is singing."

"I understand. Unfortunately, I have to work on Thursday, and on Friday we have the community meeting. I don't want to wait until Saturday to see you again, so why don't I come to the concert? We could get ice cream after."

"Really?" she asked in surprise. "You want to come to an elementary school concert? Most of the parents don't even want to come."

He laughed. "Well, I'm not a parent, so it will be more fun for me. Are you working it?"

"No, thank goodness. I'll just be in the audience."

"Then we can sit together. What time is it at?"

"It starts at six thirty. Brandon has to be there at six, so if you don't change your mind between now and then, you can meet me at the school."

"And you'll save me a seat?"

"I will," she replied, thinking it was probably the oddest second date she'd ever agreed to.

"Then I'll see you there." He pulled her in close and kissed her before she had time to wonder again if he would.

This kiss went on much longer than the last one, and the heat of their passion warmed her all the way down to her soul. She had the strangest feeling she could go on kissing Reid forever. She wanted to taste every corner of his mouth. She wanted to feel his arms around her, his hard chest against her breasts, his legs intertwined with hers. But before she could move closer, Reid lifted his head, gave her another sexy smile, then murmured, "Good-night," and walked out the door.

She was a little stunned by his abrupt departure. She watched him walk to his truck, then finally shut the door. She leaned against it, her mouth still tingling, and realized how stupid she'd been to agree to see him again. She was getting in deeper with every minute. At least tomorrow she would have a seven-year-old chaperone. That might prevent a repeat of what had just happened, although she couldn't think of anything better than having a repeat.

Shaking her head, she knew she was in trouble. She should tell him not to come. But Brandon would love having Reid in the audience. It would be nice for him to have someone besides just his mother to cheer him on.

After tomorrow, she'd end things with Reid before they got more complicated. But as she went upstairs, she had the feeling it might already be too late to avoid that.

Ten

Reid spent the early hours of dawn Wednesday morning in the surf with Bill Carlton, who'd decided to leave the beach for a change and actually get into the water.

"You're loving it again, aren't you?" he asked, as he sat on his board ten feet from Bill, waiting for the next wave.

"I did forget how much fun this was," Bill admitted, pushing his wet hair off his forehead.

Looking over his shoulder, Reid saw a wave beginning to build. "Race you to the beach."

"You're on."

For the next few minutes, it wasn't so much a race against his longtime friend as a battle against the ocean, a battle he rode out to the very end. He made it to the sand before Bill, who had wiped out earlier than him and had to swim back to shore.

He dropped his board and let out a breath. There was nothing better than surfing to start the day.

"Nice ride," Bill said. "What I saw of it, anyway. I am definitely rusty."

"You'll get it back; you just need to get out more."

"Not that easy to leave my beautiful girlfriend in bed while I hit the cold water," Bill joked.

He grinned back at him. "I get it."

"So I hear the Revolution Surfing Competition might be on next week. High surf in the forecast."

"I heard that, too," he said, thinking about the infamous surfing competition, one of the top ten competitions in the world, that took place locally when the conditions were perfect with waves cresting over twenty-five feet. "I'm thinking about giving it another shot."

Bill gave him a doubtful look. "You're not serious. You can't surf with those guys anymore."

"Hey I was a finalist at one time."

"Yeah, I think that was ten years ago, when you were twenty. Can you even get in with the pros?"

"They offer past finalists a wild card entry on the first heats. I might have been younger then, but I'm fitter now."

"You should also have more sense, more fear. You're not invincible. And you're not at the top of your game when it comes to surfing."

"I'm not looking to win, just to test myself."

Bill shook his head, giving him a resigned look. "It's always about the test with you."

"It's called pushing yourself. You should try it some time."

"I push myself plenty. I have a good life, and I don't feel like risking it on a surfboard." Bill paused, giving him a thoughtful look. "You always act like you've got nothing to lose, but I wonder if that's still true."

"What does that mean?" he asked warily, quite sure he didn't really want to know.

"You seem interested in Jessica and her son."

"They don't have anything to do with this."

"Are you dating her?"

"We had dinner last night," he admitted. "And I'm going to Brandon's concert tonight."

"Wait." Bill put up his hand. "Did you just tell me you're going to a kid's school concert?"

"It's not a big deal. I like Brandon. He reminds me of myself. I grew up without a dad. I know what that feels like."

"Then you also must know what it feels like to wonder if you'll get another dad, maybe one better than the original. But when you don't get that guy, you could end up hurt."

"Look, I know there are risks. Jessica has said the same thing to me."

"But?"

"But I like her."

"Still—I have to ask you what you're doing," Bill said, giving him a frowning look. "You've spent years telling me you don't know if you'll ever get married, that you like being single, and now you're getting involved with a woman who has a child? It doesn't make sense. I thought you wanted less responsibility, not more."

He sighed, knowing that Bill made a good point. "I can change my mind, can't I?"

"Sure, but someone could get hurt. And I'm not just talking about Jessica or Brandon; I'm talking about you, too. She's not a woman you're just going to have fun with and then move on. You know that, so if you're still interested in her…well, let's just say you could be riding for a fall."

"I'm never worried about falling. I know how to get up."

"Some things are harder to get up from."

"I know what I'm doing." He hoped that was true.

"Fine. It's your life."

"Exactly."

"I'm going to head home," Bill said, grabbing his board. "Amy is making pancakes. She said you're welcome to join us if you want."

"Thanks, but I'll pass."

"Suit yourself. Enjoy your concert tonight."

"I will."

As he walked toward the parking lot, he couldn't help but think about what Bill had said. He knew he was in dangerous water, but just like the surf he'd left behind, he wasn't afraid to challenge himself.

Maybe Jessica wasn't the kind of woman he usually dated, but he was into her and she was into him, and at the moment that's all that mattered.

"Is Reid here?" Brandon asked, as Jessica looked through the curtain at the auditorium.

"Not yet, but it's early," she replied, turning back to him. "I'm going to go out and save him a seat."

"Okay," Brandon said, an odd look in his eyes.

"What's wrong? Are you nervous about singing tonight?"

"No." Brandon licked his lips, then added, "Do you think Reid is really going to come?"

She was suddenly reminded of all the times Kevin had let Brandon down, how many times

Brandon had asked that question about his father. She didn't think Reid would bail, but she wasn't completely positive. He might have had second thoughts since last night, when he realized he'd just volunteered to sit through a kid's concert, but she hoped not.

Putting her own doubt aside, she gave Brandon a smile and said, "I'm sure he'll be here."

"Do you think Reid will think I'm good?" he asked, more insecurity in his face.

"How could he not? You're one of the best singers in the group." She actually wasn't lying about that. Brandon always seemed to hit the right note.

As the teacher in charge of the backstage area called the kids together, she gave Brandon a hug, wished him luck, and then walked into the auditorium.

There were two seats about eight rows back, so she grabbed those. While she waited for Reid, she chatted with some of her students and their parents as they walked by, feeling a bit conspicuous about her saved seat as the minutes ticked by and the auditorium filled up.

Brandon would be so disappointed if Reid didn't show, and to be honest, so would she. She'd been crazy to invite him to come to a school concert. She should have nipped this whole thing in the bud, kept it at one date. He'd just been so nice to her the night before, she hadn't wanted to say no.

Blowing out an angry breath, she was somewhat startled when Reid slipped into the aisle seat.

"Sorry I'm late," he said. "I was helping a friend move, and my truck got stuck behind the moving van, and, well, it's a long story, but I apologize."

"It's fine. You didn't miss anything."

His gaze raked her face. "You didn't think I was coming, did you?"

"I didn't know."

"Jess," he said, his blue eyes deliberate and intense. "If I say I'm going to be somewhere, I'm there. I'm not your ex-husband. Let's make that perfectly clear."

"I've never thought you were anything like Kevin," she replied.

"Good." He smiled, easing the tension between them. "How's our boy doing?"

Her heart twisted at his casual use of the words *our boy*. It had been so long since she'd felt like she had a partner on a night like this. She'd been alone at every event—until now.

"Is he nervous?" Reid pressed.

"A little. But Brandon likes a stage; I think he'll be all right. I'm nervous about his solo. It's not a long part, but he will be completely on his own."

"A solo, huh? That sounds terrifying."

She smiled. "I thought you weren't afraid of anything."

"I've never had to stand up and sing in front of this many people. Brandon is very brave."

"Or too young to be worried," she said. "I, on the other hand, really want him to do well."

"He will."

As the lights dimmed, Reid grabbed her hand, squeezing his fingers around hers.

She was shocked at how long it had been since a man had held her hand and even more shocked at how much she liked it—so much, she couldn't let go.

And that's how they watched the concert, hand-in-hand, sharing soft, sometimes joking comments during the show. And when Brandon came out to sing with his group, Reid tightened his grip on her hand, as if he was as nervous for Brandon to do well as she was.

In the end, there was nothing to have been nervous about. Brandon hit every note in his short solo and she and Reid finally let go of each other to add their applause to the enthusiastic support from the audience. She could see Brandon searching for her and probably for Reid, so she waved to him. His smile broadened, and then he disappeared behind the curtain.

"Amazing," Reid whispered to her, as he took her hand again.

"He was, wasn't he?"

"He sang like a little angel. His tone was so pure."

"I don't know where he gets the talent, but it's definitely there."

"Maybe he'll grow up to be a singer—a rock star."

She laughed. "That's a worry for another day."

He grinned. "Don't tell me it hadn't already crossed your mind."

She couldn't do that, because as a mom she imagined Brandon's future all the time, and hearing him sing had made her think about what he could do with that voice. "I have thought about it," she admitted. "But there's a limit to how much I can worry about at any one time."

"I'm glad to hear there's a limit," he said dryly.

"The next act is coming out," she said as a fifth-grader walked out with her cello.

"I can't believe kids still play those," Reid muttered.

She smiled, then winced as the child hit a particularly rough note to start, but she got better after that and by the end of the song, she was doing really well.

"Not as bad as you thought," she murmured.

"You're right. She made me a cello lover," he replied.

"Did you ever play an instrument?"

He shook his head. "No. I played a toy guitar that went with a video game, but that was about it. You?"

"The flute. My mom thought it was classy. I imagined she pictured me in a long evening gown, playing the flute in an orchestra, but I was terrible at it. And forcing me to play did not make me better. I think it's great to expose kids to instruments, but they have to find a love for it, or it's just not going to work." She fell silent as the next act came onto the stage. Four hip-hop dancers brought some new energy to the concert, which continued into the grand finale, with all the kids coming on stage to sing a song and take their bows.

When the show was over and the lights went up, Brandon came running down the aisle from the stage. The happiness on his face when he saw Reid almost made her want to cry. There would be no disappointment tonight. Of course, watching them exchange a hug confirmed her fears that Brandon already liked Reid too much, but she couldn't change any of that now.

"I was good, wasn't I, Mommy?" Brandon said, finally turning to her.

She hugged him close. "Very good, honey. Let's go outside. We're blocking the aisle."

Brandon received compliments from some of his

friends' parents as they moved through the auditorium. Finally, they made it outside and into the parking lot. Since she and Brandon had come early, she had a good parking spot not too far away.

"My car is right there," she said, waving her hand toward her white Honda CRV.

"You're lucky. I'm about three blocks away," Reid said.

"Did you really think I was good, Reid?" Brandon asked again.

"I think you stole the show," Reid said.

Brandon's smile grew wider. "Jenny forgot the chorus, and she said she was going to be the star, but she wasn't."

"Brandon, that isn't nice," she said.

"It's true," Brandon said.

Reid laughed. "I take it Jenny is some sort of nemesis."

"She's a very pretty, queen-bee second-grader. She's good at everything and she likes to share that as often as she can," Jessica said.

"But I was better than her tonight," Brandon boasted.

"It's not about being better than someone else. It's just about doing your best," she said, knowing that her words were probably falling on deaf ears. Brandon was too caught up in his own success to see the bigger picture, so she'd let him have his moment.

"Can we get ice cream?" Brandon asked. "My friends are going to Sweet Treats."

"It will be packed, honey," she said. Not only did she want to avoid the crowd, she preferred to avoid questions about Reid from some of her fellow teachers and the parents of her students.

"But I want ice cream," Brandon complained. "You said Reid was going to take us to get some."

"How about this?" Reid interrupted. "I'll go by the store on the way to your house and pick up whatever ice cream you want, along with hot fudge sauce, whipped cream, nuts, cherries, bananas, and we can go crazy making sundaes at your house."

"Okay," Brandon said happily.

Reid's gaze swung to hers. "All right with you, Jess?"

"Sure," she said. "I can't say no to ice cream sundaes." Actually, she couldn't say no to him, but it was probably best not to tell him that.

"I'll see you both in a few minutes."

As Reid left, Brandon slipped his hand into hers as they walked to the car.

"I like Reid," Brandon said.

"Me, too," she murmured.

"Do you think he likes me?"

"Of course he does. He wouldn't have come to your concert if he didn't." She opened the back door of her car.

As Brandon hopped inside, he said, "Does Reid have a girlfriend?"

"I don't think so."

"Maybe you could be his girlfriend. He likes you, too, I can tell."

"Reid and I are just friends. That's all," she said, pretty sure that was the first lie she'd ever told her son.

Jessica liked whipped cream as much as Brandon did, Reid thought, smiling to himself as Jessica wiped the tip of her nose and gave a guilty laugh.

While Brandon's sundae had been kept fairly simple, for Jessica and himself he'd made two magnificently decadent sundaes with multiple scoops of ice cream, hot fudge sauce, whipped cream, nuts, and a cherry on top, and Jessica had eaten every bit of hers. He liked seeing her laugh and be spontaneous and ignore the fact that she'd just swallowed thousands of calories. She could be serious and worry about far too many things, but he wondered if that was because she had so much on her own shoulders.

What if someone stepped up and took some of that burden away?

But was he that someone? He certainly hadn't been in the past.

"I haven't indulged like this in a while," Jessica said, sitting back in her seat. "I cannot believe I ate all that."

"It's good to let loose once in a—" He was interrupted by a crash. He looked past the kitchen island to the family room, where Brandon and a barking Wiley had just knocked over a lamp.

"Sorry, Mommy," Brandon said quickly.

Jessica got up to right the lamp. "It's okay, but you and Wiley need to settle down," she added. "Why don't you go upstairs, brush your teeth, and get into your pajamas?"

"Will you read stories with me again, Reid?" Brandon asked.

"Sure," Reid said.

"Maybe one," she interjected. "It's getting late."

"Pick out whatever book you want," he said. "I'll be up in a few minutes."

"Okay," Brandon replied, running out of the room

with a barking Wiley at his heels.

"So the kid is a little pumped up on sugar," he said with a grin.

"You think? I knew the sundaes were a bad idea." She got up and took her empty bowl to the sink.

"But they were good," he said, following her to the counter.

"They were," she agreed. "A lot of bad ideas are good for the short-term but bad for the long-term."

"I don't think we're talking about ice cream anymore."

As she turned, he put his hands on either side of her, trapping her between the counter and him.

"I have another bad idea," he murmured, inhaling the sweet scent of her skin.

He lifted a hand and ran his fingers through the thick waves of her hair, cupping the side of her face, his thumb drifting down her cheek.

Her eyes darkened, and he heard a catch in her breath. Her lips parted, and it was just too sweet of an invitation to resist. He lowered his head, taking his time, wanting to savor every second, because he didn't know how many seconds he'd have. The touch of her mouth under his tightened every muscle in his body and jolted every nerve.

She tasted like chocolate and cream, her lips soft and yielding. She might fight him with her words, but she wasn't fighting now. She was kissing him back with a sensual, tentative shyness that grew bolder as her tongue tangled with his. Her arms came around his back, and he rejoiced in the feel of her body moving even closer.

She tilted her head one way, then the other. When he thought about stopping, she pulled him back in.

When she thought about stopping, he did the same.

It wasn't enough to just kiss her. He wanted his hands on the curvy breasts he could feel against his chest. He wanted his fingers on her bare skin. He wanted to feel the curve of her hips under his. He wanted…so much…

"Reid," she said breathlessly, breaking the kiss. "I…" She looked into his eyes.

"Me, too," he said, seeing the desire there.

"I don't know what to do."

"Neither do I," he said softly, liking that they were on the same page for at least a moment.

And then Brandon's sharp voice cut into the moment, reminding him that with Jessica, it was never going to just be about the two of them.

"Mommy, Reid," Brandon yelled. "I'm ready for my story."

Jessica slipped away from him, walking over to the door and yelling back, "We'll be there in a minute. Get in bed."

He drew in a breath, trying to get his head back in the game. Then he turned to face Jessica.

She folded her arms across her chest, as if she needed the barrier between them. "You don't have to read to him. I can do it."

"I said I would. I keep my promises."

"You've already gone above and beyond, Reid. Just going to the concert meant a lot to him."

"I had a good time." He walked across the room. "I had a better time a few seconds ago."

Her eyes sparkled with his words. "I did, too."

"I know you did. So how about a third date?"

"You're pushing your luck."

"I didn't hear a no."

"I should say no," she murmured.

"But you're going to say yes."

"I'm still thinking."

"Think about how you felt a few minutes ago. I'm going to read Brandon his story." He'd no sooner finished speaking when his phone rang. He pulled it out of his pocket, surprised when he saw the number for the police department. "I have to get this," he said. "Hello?" He couldn't believe what he was hearing. "This doesn't sound right. Tara doesn't do things like this." He paused, forced to listen again. "Okay, I'll be right there."

Jessica gave him a questioning look. "Who was that?"

"The police department. My sister Tara has been arrested."

"What? Why?"

"I don't know exactly. Something about drinking and vandalism. I have to go down there."

"Of course you do."

His lips tightened as Brandon let out another impatient call from upstairs. "I'm sorry, Jess, I can't—"

"Don't even worry about it."

"I don't want to disappoint him."

"He'll be fine. Go. Take care of your sister. And let me know if you need anything."

Eleven

"I need to lay down," Tara said, as she flopped onto Reid's couch.

"You need a hell of a lot more than that," he retorted. "I can't believe you, Tara. What were you thinking?"

She gave him a pained, teary look, her mascara streaked across her face, her skin pale from multiple episodes of vomiting. Curled up on his couch, she looked a lot younger than her almost eighteen years of age. In fact, right now she reminded him of when she'd been seven and sick with the flu and he'd been watching her while their mom was at a party. He'd felt really bad for her then, wanting to make her feel better. He felt bad for her now, too, but he was also angry.

"Well?" he demanded, sitting on the edge of the recliner next to the couch. "What made you think shooting tequila, running around downtown, and trying to steal a stop sign was a good idea?"

"We were just fooling around," she muttered. "Can you yell at me tomorrow? I don't feel good."

Forever Starts Tonight

"Oh, believe me, I'll be yelling at you for a while—tonight, tomorrow, next week. I don't think you understand how serious this is. You were not only drinking and underage—you were arrested for vandalizing public property."

"It wasn't my idea. Tawny said since we couldn't get the sign down, we should just change it."

"Who bought the spray paint?"

"Doug."

"Whose idea was it to write on the sign?"

"I don't know." She put a hand to her mouth. "I think I'm going to be sick again."

"You know where the bathroom is. I'd try to make sure you aim well, because you'll be cleaning it up."

"Why are you being so mean? Like you never did anything wrong?"

"I didn't do anything this stupid. You have college waiting for you. They could rescind your acceptance because of this."

She shrugged. "Whatever. It doesn't matter."

"Of course it matters. You told me you were excited to go to San Diego State." He paused. "This is about Mom, isn't it? Did you think she might come home if she found out you were arrested?"

"I'm not stupid enough to think that. I was just partying with my friends. The sign was a bad idea, but it was a joke."

He let out a sigh, happy in a small way that her rebellious night hadn't ended up on a worse note. His friends at the police department had told him that she and her friends would have to pay a fine and do some community service, but her crime wouldn't have a long-lasting consequence. He hoped not, because he knew this wasn't the kind of stuff his sister normally did. She was just hurting.

"Did you tell Mom what I did?" Tara asked.

He shook his head. "I'm going to let you do that. You can text her."

"I don't want to do it now."

"Why not? She might come home. This dose of hard reality might shake her out of her romantic dazed stupor."

"I don't want her to come home because she has to. She should want to be here with me. I'm her kid. She's supposed to take care of me until I graduate from high school."

"I agree, Tara, but Mom just doesn't follow the rule book. She loves you, but she doesn't show it the way she should. She's the kind of person who's distracted by shiny new objects. She can't seem to stop chasing them. But that doesn't mean she doesn't care about you or me."

"You always make excuses for her. Your words used to make me feel better, but I'm not a kid anymore, Reid. I don't believe in Santa Claus or the Tooth Fairy or Mom's good intentions."

"I know. But along with your maturity, I hope you can find some way to forgive her. Because being angry at Mom doesn't hurt her; it hurts you. I don't want you to be hurt anymore."

"How did you stop being mad?"

He thought about her question. "I realized that you needed a brother, and being mad at Mom wouldn't have allowed us to have a relationship, so I had to put my anger on the back burner. Not that she still doesn't drive me crazy, but I try to accept that that's just who she is." He paused. "You're going to have a great life, Tara. You have everything ahead of you—college, new friends, probably boyfriends I'm going to hate."

She made a face at him.

"And then you'll graduate," he continued. "You'll find a career for yourself. You'll travel. You'll get married one day. It's all going to be good. Mom is always going to be Mom. But you can be whoever you want to be. Don't let her hold you back. Let her be what drives you forward."

Tara stared back at him, her eyes thoughtful. "You're right. I can't let her hold me back, not when she's moving on with her own life."

"I think one reason why she's gotten caught up in the yoga and the meditation and this new man is because she's afraid of being alone when you're gone."

"She's barely with me now."

"But you're there. You're in the house when she's around. And she's never been good at good-byes or being alone. But whatever happens with her and this guy, it's not going to affect the rest of your life. You're not going to let it, are you?"

"No." She licked her lips. "I'm sorry, Reid. I was stupid."

"You were, and you're still going to tell Mom what you did."

She snuggled down into the couch and closed her eyes. "In the morning."

He got up and grabbed a blanket from the closet and put it over her, then went into his room. He took out his phone, then hesitated when he saw it was after eleven. It was too late to call Jessica. He'd have to talk to her tomorrow.

He'd no sooner set his phone down on the bed when it pinged. His heart lightened when her name popped up in his text messages.

Everything okay? she asked. *How's your sister?*

Fine. Going to have a hell of a hangover. She deserves it.

Tough love, huh?

She was stupid tonight.

Teenagers are often stupid. Glad I have some time before Brandon turns into one.

You'll be ready. So when do I get a third date?

We'll see.

He put his phone away. She hadn't said no; he'd take that as a win. He didn't know what was going to happen between them, but he definitely wanted to find out.

She'd missed him. *How ridiculous was that?* It had only been two and a half days since she'd seen Reid, but it felt much longer than that. And when she walked into the high school for her second and final community emergency prep class Friday night, she felt her heart beating a little faster at the thought of seeing him again.

They'd texted a few times, but between his job and her job, and Brandon's activities, there hadn't been time for anything more. He'd mentioned getting together on the weekend, but they'd made no definite plans, mostly because she still hadn't committed to seeing him again, even though, of course, she wanted to.

When she turned the corner, she saw Reid in the hall outside the gym, talking to one of the other students, and nervous butterflies in her stomach went into a free fall. He was even more handsome in his uniform, if that were possible.

When he finished his conversation and turned his gaze on her, he gave her what felt like a very personal and intimate smile that was just for her.

Every time he looked at her like that, she felt the hard wall she'd built around her heart begin to crack. She was letting him into her life, into Brandon's life, one date at a time. It was risky, but she couldn't seem to stop herself from saying yes to him. She kept telling herself one more time, one more night, one more date, but at some point, she had to end it, didn't she?

But that wasn't going to be tonight. Tonight she had to be here. It was part of her job.

"Hi," he said, coming down the hall to greet her. He took a quick look around and then gave her a quick kiss.

She flushed a little. "You're not supposed to kiss your students."

"Good thing I'm not a real teacher. I missed you, Jess."

Her stomach clenched. "It hasn't been that long."

"Hasn't it? Who's staying with Brandon tonight?"

"Hayley from across the street."

"Do you have time for coffee after class?"

"Unfortunately, no. I promised Hayley I'd be back by ten. She's going to New York tomorrow with her parents and their flight leaves at seven a.m."

"That's early. So, tonight doesn't work, but we have the weekend coming up. You said you'd think about a third date. What are you doing tomorrow?"

"Well, here's the thing," she began.

He smiled. "Okay, I'm listening."

"My college friends, the ones I told you about,

have an annual pizza-making competition every year. I haven't been able to go in years, because I was too far away, so they pretty much made me promise to come tomorrow. It's in San Francisco. I'm taking Brandon and a friend of his, so he has someone to play with." She paused, hoping she wasn't making a big mistake. "If you want to come with me, we could do that. But if you don't, I completely understand."

"I can handle pizza and meeting your friends."

"Really? I have to warn you that they'll probably grill you about dating me."

"As long as you now acknowledge that we're dating, I can handle it."

She frowned, realizing she'd tripped herself up.

He laughed. "Don't worry. It will be fine. We'll tell your friends whatever you want. What time?"

"It starts around five. It takes an hour to get there—so four?"

"Perfect. I'll pick you up then."

"Okay. We better head inside. You can't be late for your own class."

"Good point."

She followed Reid into the gym and saw Paula sitting in the third row of the stands. She sat down next to her and they chatted for a few moments as Reid, Bill, and two police officers set up their presentation. For the next three hours, her attention was focused solely on becoming a good citizen responder in a number of intense emergency situations.

At the first class, she hadn't known Reid well enough to appreciate how good he was at his job, but tonight she saw him in full-on serious mode. There was no trace of the happy-go-lucky surfer who liked to take life as it came. He took his job seriously and he impressed upon them the need to do the same.

It was interesting to see another side of him. Unfortunately, it only made her like him more. She was supposed to be looking for reasons not to see him again, not the other way around.

When the class was over, she debated between waiting for everyone to leave so she could have another minute or two with Reid or head on out. He was in a conversation with one of the city council members, which could take a long time, and she did only have about fifteen minutes before she had to get home.

As she was debating, Bill Carlton came over to her. "How's it going?"

"Good. The class was great. Very informative."

"I'm happy to hear that. How did Brandon like his tour of the firehouse?"

"He loved it. He's decided he's going to be a firefighter—at least for now."

"Good to hear." He paused. "So are you going to watch Reid take on the big waves in the Revolution Surfing Competition?"

"What's that?"

"It's a big surfing event. The best surfers in the world come to Half Moon Bay when the conditions are exactly right and the forecast anticipates those conditions coming end of next week."

"What kind of conditions?"

"Twenty-five foot waves."

Her stomach churned as she pictured a surfer trying to take on a wave of that size. "And Reid wants to compete?"

"Yes. He was a finalist a long time ago.

Apparently, he's decided to relive his glory days."

"Is Reid that good?"

"Am I that good at what?" Reid asked, interrupting their conversation. "And before you tell me, I'm sure the answer is yes."

"Cocky as usual," Bill said with a laugh. "We were talking about you possibly surfing Revolution next week."

"Are you really going to do it?" she asked, surprised by how much she didn't like the idea.

"I haven't decided yet. They give former finalists a wild card. It's up to me whether or not I want to take it."

"When did you final in the competition?"

"About ten years ago."

"That's a long time," she said. "Don't you need to practice for this kind of thing?"

"I go out all the time."

"But not against waves like these," Bill put in.

"Thanks, Bill. You can say good-night now," Reid said to his friend.

"Good-night," Bill said obediently, then walked away.

"You don't have to worry, Jessica," Reid told her.

She didn't know what she needed to do. She certainly didn't want to add more worry to her life. "I should get going."

"We're still on for tomorrow, right?" Reid asked, following her outside.

"I don't know," she said with a sigh.

"Jess, wait." He put a hand on her arm, making her stop walking to look at him. "What's wrong? You're really bothered that I want to participate in the surfing competition? Why?"

"I guess I don't understand why you'd want to risk your life to ride a wave."

He stared back at her. "It's not about the wave. It's about pushing myself, really living, not just surviving."

"You already risk your life on your job. Why do you have to do it on your off time, too?"

"Jessica, one thing I've learned on the job—you can be having the most normal day in the world and something could happen and you could die. Or you could be walking a tightrope between two skyscrapers and not die. I don't live my life scared."

"But there's a difference between not doing anything and being reckless."

"You're right. And maybe surfing this competition again is not a good idea. I haven't made a decision yet. I don't even know if it will happen. They often call it off if the conditions aren't right. I'll decide when I need to make a decision."

She thought about his words for a moment, feeling like she did live her life scared, but she was a mom. She couldn't take risks for herself anymore. She had to consider Brandon.

"You're thinking too much," Reid said. "You're always three steps ahead in your mind, aren't you?"

"Yes, but that's because I have to protect Brandon. I don't have just myself to think about. I have to be more cautious. I'm all he has."

"I understand, and I promise not to ask you to ride the waves with me."

"Like that would ever happen."

"So what about tomorrow? I'm still going to pizza, right? I don't think anyone can get hurt there, unless the pizza slicer rolls out of someone's hand,

and—"

"Stop," she said, knowing he was teasing her. "Yes, you're going to pizza night. And, yes, I know I can be too serious. Believe it or not, worrying exhausts me, but I don't always know how to stop."

"Well, you don't have to worry about me."

That was easier said than done, because she was starting to care about him, starting to want him in her life and in Brandon's.

Reid put his arm around her shoulders, and as they walked out to her car, she thought about what he'd said about her always being three steps ahead, and she realized how true that was. Maybe she should make a better effort to live in the moment.

When they got to her car, she put her arms around his neck and pulled his head down, taking the kiss she wanted, the one she'd been thinking about every second of the class.

His mouth and his arms were a heated haven and she never wanted to leave. He'd not only stirred up her emotions, he'd stirred up her desires. She was falling fast…she just didn't want a hard landing. But as Reid had just said, life was for living, not just surviving. For tonight, she'd put her worries on hold.

"I'll see you tomorrow," she said, pulling away from him.

He groaned. "You're slowly killing me, Jess. I hope you know that."

She liked that he was as caught up in her as she was in him. "Good-night, Reid."

"Happy dreams."

She got into her car and shut the door, quite sure her dreams were going to be happy, and they were going to be about him.

Twelve

"So tell me about your friends," Reid said, as he drove away from her house with Brandon and his friend Joel in the backseat.

The boys were sharing headphones as they watched a video on her tablet. That should keep them busy for the hour-long drive to the city.

"Well, let's see," she replied. "We're going to Andrea's house. She's married to Alex Donovan."

"The billionaire videogame maker? Seriously?" he asked, giving her a questioning look.

"Yes. He's that Alex Donovan. He's very wealthy, but he's also a great guy. He came from nothing. He truly is a self-made man, and I think you'll find him down-to-earth and easy to talk to."

"How did Alex and Andrea meet?"

"She's a journalist and she was sent to interview him for a magazine. She was trying to find some dirt on him, but she couldn't, and they wound up falling in love. Their house is in Presidio Heights, and it's amazing. They have an enormous game room with all the latest videogames. Alex is very active with underprivileged kids, and he invites a lot of them over to the house to test out new games. He said he'd set Brandon and Joel up with enough fun to keep them busy for hours."

"Sounds cool. I'd like to see some of those games myself."

She laughed. "I'm sure you will."

"Who else will be there?"

"Liz and her husband Michael Stafford are coming. Michael used to play professional football, then he got hurt and went into public relations. He found himself competing with Liz, who was with a rival firm, for a client. The funny thing is that they knew each other in high school, and they'd been competing as teenagers in school, so it was the revival of an old rivalry."

"Who won the competition?"

"In the end, they wound up getting the client together, but I think technically Liz might have won. After that, Michael actually got a job coaching football, so he's mostly doing that now. Then there is Julie and her husband, Matt Kingsley."

"Wait? What? Matt Kingsley—as in the star of Cougars baseball?"

She laughed. "Yes, that Matt Kingsley."

"This party is really shaping up—new video games, pro baseball players, former pro football players; I think I like your friends."

"The women are just as important as the guys," she said pointedly. "Andrea is working in television news now. She's done some amazing whistle-blowing stories that have shaken things up in Washington. Julie runs Matt's charity foundation, so she does good works in a different way, and Liz is co-owner of the

PR firm she shares with Michael."

"Sorry, I didn't mean they weren't important," Reid said.

"I know, but I just wanted to clarify. Kate is also coming, maybe with a date. She's the only other single one in the group besides me, which is ironic, since she's a wedding planner."

"Your group must be giving her a lot of business."

"Absolutely. Andrea and Liz are the two who are also pregnant."

"Is that it?"

"Andrea's twin sister Laurel and her husband Greg should be there. Isabella and her fiancé Nick might come late. I know Maggie out; she's the one who lives in Napa, so that's the group."

"What kind of pizza are we making? I noticed some interesting ingredients in the bags you asked me to put in the back of the car."

"You inspired me to be adventurous," she said with a smile.

"Okay, now I'm scared."

"I doubt that. We're going to do a grilled honey siracha chicken pizza."

"I have never heard of that."

"I found a recipe and a picture that looked amazing, so I thought why not? It's a good time to try it out. Go big or go home."

He laughed. "Okay, I like this new risk-taking Jessica."

She was starting to like her, too. The new Jessica actually felt a little like the old Jessica, the woman she'd been before Kevin and Brandon. Somewhere along the way, she'd lost that girl, but maybe she was getting her back. And if she was, it probably had a lot to do with Reid.

He hadn't been to San Francisco in a few weeks, and it was fun to get back into the city, although he'd certainly never spent a lot of time in the neighborhood of Presidio Heights where stately mansions lined the block. He wasn't quite sure what to expect from Alex and Andrea, but as soon as he stepped into their impressive home, he was given a warm greeting by both of them.

"I hope we're not late," Jessica said after making the introductions.

"Not at all," Andrea replied. "Michael and Liz, Julie and Matt, and Laurel and Greg are here. Kate is on her way. Isabella and Nick are probably not going to make their own pizza but will be here to eat later."

"I didn't know that was an option," Reid joked.

Alex gave him a commiserating smile. "Andrea didn't tell me that, either."

"You love making the pizza," Andrea told her husband.

"Do I?" Alex countered with a laugh.

Andrea gave her husband a playful punch in the arm. "He's just joking," she told them.

"So," Jessica began, turning to Alex. "Congratulations. Andrea told me the exciting news last weekend."

Alex beamed as he put his arm around his pretty blonde wife. "Thanks. We're beyond thrilled."

"At least we are in between bouts of morning sickness," Andrea put in. "Liz has had no nausea whatsoever. It is not fair at all."

"That's Liz—always cool, calm and collected," Jessica said.

"Exactly. It's annoying. Anyway, come on back to the kitchen."

"I'll show the boys to the game room," Alex said, turning to Brandon and Joel. "Are you two ready to play some games?"

"I want to play Wing Rider," Brandon said, naming one of Alex's most popular games.

"Of course. You can play anything you want." He paused as a boy of about fifteen came down the hall. "Tyler, just the guy I need. This is Brandon and Joel; this is Tyler. He's going to set you up on whatever games you want to play."

"Follow me," Tyler said.

"Okay, Mommy?" Brandon asked.

Jessica nodded. "Have fun. I'll call you when the pizzas are ready."

As the boys left, Alex said, "Tyler will make sure they have a good time and that they don't get into any trouble."

"I appreciate the babysitter and the video games," Jessica said.

"Happy to do it. And I'm happy to have your son try out a new game I'm working on for his age group. Tyler will show him that when he's done with Wing Rider."

"He'll be over the moon," Jessica said, as they followed Andrea and Alex down the hall to an enormous gourmet kitchen that opened onto an even larger family room with a big screen television that took up one wall.

Reid was happy to see the Golden State Warriors

were up in the first quarter of the basketball game.

"Nice TV," he muttered, unable to keep the awe from his voice.

"It's obscene," Andrea put in. "But it was here before I was, so it stayed."

Alex laughed. "You love watching your shows on it, too, Andrea."

"I'll never admit that," she said.

As they moved into the kitchen, Reid was introduced to Michael and Liz. Liz was a brown-eyed blonde with a very suspicious gaze. He also met Julie and Matt. Julie gave him a sweet smile, and Matt extended a hand for a hearty handshake. The third couple, Laurel and Greg, were already up to their elbows in dough.

"Laurel is making her dough from scratch," Andrea said. "My twin sister likes to win."

"That's your twin?" Reid said in surprise. The brunette didn't look anything like Andrea.

"Fraternal," Laurel sang out, giving him a smile. "Nice to meet you. And I don't see the point of competing if you don't want to win."

"Jessica wants to win, too," Reid put in.

"What are you making, Jess?" Andrea asked curiously.

"It's a secret," she said, giving him a warning look. "No hints until we serve it."

"I won't say a word," he promised.

"Well, find a spot anywhere and do what you need to do," Andrea said. "We'll have to cook the pizzas in shifts."

He set down their grocery bags on a nearby counter as Liz came around the island to speak to them.

"So what do you do, Reid?" she asked.

"I'm a firefighter."

"That sounds dangerous."

"It can be, but we also go on a lot of non-dangerous calls—cats up in trees, women stuck in doghouses." He saw Jessica's cheeks flush at his words.

"Women stuck in doghouses?" Liz asked doubtfully. "You're joking, right?"

"I'm actually not. It happened quite recently," he said. "We never know what we're going to run into when we go out on a call."

"Reid also surfs," Jessica put in, obviously wanting to change the subject.

"No kidding," Michael said, joining his wife while Alex and Matt moved into the family room to watch the game. "I used to surf out in Half Moon Bay when I was a teenager."

"We probably met on the waves," he said. "Do you still go out?"

"Not in years. I heard on the news that they're trying to hold the Revolution competition next week. I was thinking about going out there. Did you ever surf those waves?"

"A long time ago. I got to the last heat, but I didn't win."

"That's still impressive. Would you do it again?"

"Not sure I'll have the opportunity, but I wouldn't rule it out."

"Do you have a death wish or something?" Liz asked. "Fires, big waves—sounds like a man who likes to challenge fate."

"Not fate—just myself," he said easily, not taking offense, because he could clearly see that Liz was sizing him up. Andrea was paying attention, too, and Julie had moved closer to get in on their conversation as well.

"How did you and Jessica meet?" Andrea asked curiously.

"Reid is teaching a community emergency prep class that I had to go to for school," Jessica answered quickly, sending him a warning look.

He smiled, having no intention of outing her doghouse adventure. "I had to teach her how to triage in case of a community-wide emergency," he said.

"You mean, like pick who lives and dies?" Julie asked with a frown. "That doesn't sound fun."

"It wasn't fun, but it was informative and important," Jessica said.

"But then we went out to dinner, and that was fun," he put in. "This is actually our third date—make that fourth if we count Brandon's school concert. I'm hoping for a fifth."

"Reid," Jessica said, with an embarrassed smile. "You don't have to tell them that."

"They want to know if I'm good enough for you, and I don't blame them," he said, smiling at her friends. "Ask me anything you want; my life is an open book."

"Don't tell them that," Michael said with a laugh. "These women do not need encouragement to ask questions."

"I can take it."

"Questions can wait," Jessica said firmly. "We need to start cooking. Reid is right. I am interested in winning. I've been hearing about these competitions the last few years, and I finally get to be in one, so I'm going for the gold."

"You know there's not really any gold, right?" Liz drawled.

Jessica grinned. "Beating all of you will be enough."

"Don't get so cocky," Laurel put in. "Greg and I are going to shock you with our pizza."

"Maybe we should have bought more than pepperoni and onions," Michael told Liz.

"We got more than that," she said.

"We did? What are we making?"

"It's a surprise," Liz said, taking her husband's hand. "Let's get started. I can't let Jessica beat me."

"Of course you can't," Michael said dryly. "I'm going to need more wine for this."

"We have plenty of that," Andrea said. "Help yourselves. I'll let you guys go in the first round. Julie and I will go second, and Kate, once she gets here."

As Andrea and Julie moved into the family room to join their husbands, Reid moved closer to Jessica. "What can I do to help?"

"You can start chopping the vegetables. I'm going to grill the chicken strips I cut up earlier."

"You're prepared."

"I usually am. As you said, I'm often three steps ahead."

"Well, maybe that will bring us a victory today."

"I like how you use the word *us*," she said with a laugh.

"I will do whatever I can to help or at least not do harm."

"I'm going to hold you to that."

As he started chopping the onions, he said, "So if you can see three steps ahead, what do you think is going to happen when I take you home tonight, after we drop off Joel, and Brandon goes up to his room?"

She shook her head, her eyes shooting out a warning. "Talk like that is not going to get you a fourth date. And Joel is spending the night."

"Fifth date," he corrected.

"You can't count the first day at the beach."

"But I can," he said. "You didn't answer my question."

"And I'm not going to."

"Fine, but I bet you're going to think about it."

Her eyes gleamed with his words, and he knew her thoughts were taking the same path as his. Well, maybe not the same path. Jess was cautious. She wasn't going to jump into anything even if she really wanted to, not unless she felt sure neither she nor Brandon would get hurt.

He wished he could promise that. But he couldn't. He frowned, thinking now he was the one who was getting too far ahead.

Thirty minutes later, their pizza was in one of the double ovens, while Laurel and Greg's pizza was in the other. Liz and Michael were waiting for one of the pizzas to come out so they could put theirs in, and Julie, Matt, Andrea, and Alex were starting their prep work.

While Jessica went to check on Brandon, he walked onto the patio outside the family room to get some fresh air. He was joined a moment later by Liz.

"You're leaving your pizza unattended," he joked.

"Michael is watching it like a hawk," she said, a sparkle in her eyes. "The one you and Jessica made looks very good. It's going to be a battle."

"If the pizzas are all good, we'll all win."

"Sure." She paused. "So what's the deal with you

two?"

"I like Jess. She likes me. That's the deal."

"But it's not just Jess—there's Brandon."

"I like Brandon, too."

"But you're a surfer and a firefighter. It doesn't really sound like you're a family man—no offense. I just want Jessica to be happy, and she's had a rough time the last few years. I don't want to see her go through any more heartache." Liz flung a quick glance over her shoulder to make sure they were alone. "She'd kill me for saying anything, but she's an amazing person, and she deserves someone equally amazing."

He liked that Liz was protective of Jess. She was sticking her nose where it didn't belong, but her heart was in the right place. "I agree with you. Jess is very special. She's also very capable of handling her own life, making her own decisions."

"I know, but sometimes love can be blinding. The man she was with, Brandon's father, he wasn't a good guy. He acted like he was, but he was selfish."

"I'm not him."

"Okay."

"Are we good?"

She smiled. "As long as you treat her well, we're good. So what do you want to ask me about Jessica?"

"Nothing," he said, surprised by the question.

"Really? You don't want to know her secrets?"

He shook his head. "That would take the fun out of finding out for myself."

She nodded approvingly. "Excellent point. I'm starting to see why Jessica likes you."

"What's going on out here?" Jessica interrupted, joining them on the patio.

He put his arm around her shoulders. "Just getting to know Liz."

"Actually, I offered to tell him some of your secrets, but he shut me down," Liz said.

"Thank goodness for that," Jessica said with a laugh.

"I better go check on my pizza and make sure Michael is still watching over it," Liz said, leaving them alone.

"So how badly did she grill you?" Jessica asked, giving him an inquisitive smile.

"She just wanted to make sure I knew you were too important to mess around with. But I already knew that."

Her eyes grew somber. "I keep telling myself that the last thing we should do is make anything too important, but…"

"But?" he prodded.

"But it feels like this is more than just fun." She looked like she wanted to say more, but they heard squeals from inside the house. She glanced toward the windows. "Looks like Kate and Isabella are here. We should go inside."

"To be continued," he said.

"Or maybe just leave it alone. I had kind of forgotten about fun until I met you. I'm enjoying being in the moment."

"Me, too, and I have a lot more fun to show you. Just give me a chance."

Thirteen

Reid got along really well with her friends, Jessica thought as she helped Kate tidy up the kitchen several hours later. They'd eaten every last crumb of six incredibly unique and excellent pizzas while sharing lots of stories. Some of those stories had been for Reid's benefit, a few too many about her life in college, but she couldn't really complain. It felt kind of good for Reid to know she hadn't always been a super serious person; she'd just grown into one.

Reid was now in the family room, telling stories from fire scenes that had the group enthralled. He was the kind of person who fit in anywhere he went.

"You picked a winner," Kate said, joining her at the kitchen island. "Reid is a man's man and a ladies' man. The guys want to be him. The women want to be with someone like him."

She couldn't deny either of Kate's statements. Because she certainly liked being with him.

Kate turned her speculative blue-eyed gaze on her. "The question for you is—what exactly do you want to do with him?"

"So many things," she said with a laugh.

Kate grinned. "Good to know. I don't think I've seen you this relaxed in a very long time, Jessica."

"I'm always relaxed when I'm with you guys."

"Somewhat, but you never really let go. You're always worrying about Brandon or getting back somewhere on time."

"The life of a single mom who happens to also be a worrier. And that trait started long before I ever met Kevin."

"That's true; you did worry a lot when we were in college." She paused. "I never thought Kevin was good for you. It wasn't like he was overtly bad, but he always seemed to stress you out. You were always trying to be the girl he wanted."

"Was I?" she asked. "I almost can't remember those days, not that there were many of them. We only went out for three months before I got pregnant. And then we leapt into marriage to appease our parents, to do what was right. After Brandon was born, it was all about taking care of him. There never seemed to be a time when there wasn't any stress." She paused. "It's weird, but since Reid came into my life, I feel like my laugh is back."

"It is back. He makes you smile."

"That's because his smile is so damned irresistible."

"He is charming and good-looking. And he seems to really like you. I think you should keep him around."

"I like him, too. I just don't know if he's really ready to take on me and Brandon and all our baggage."

"I doubt he'd keep seeing you if he wasn't ready."

"I don't know about that. Reid likes to live in the moment. He doesn't look too far down the road."

"Maybe that's a good thing."

"I'm trying to look at it that way. Let's change the subject. How is your life?"

"Business is booming, as you know."

"I'm not talking about business, but about you. After all, you and I are the last two single girls standing. Are you seeing anyone?"

"No time for that. And most people I see are happily married couples, mixed in with a few bridezillas."

"I'm sure," she said. "But you should make some time for fun."

"I will. Right now my business is my fun. I'm getting to do what I love and that's all that matters."

"I'm glad." She finished wiping down the counter, then put the towel aside. "I should probably find Brandon and wrap this evening up."

"Congrats on making the best pizza, by the way."

"Thanks," she said, happy her pizza had been voted number one by her friends.

"You're not still talking about your win, are you?" Liz interrupted, as she joined them.

She laughed. "You came in second. You should be happy."

"Second is the first loser," Liz said.

Jessica rolled her eyes. "It's just pizza, Liz."

"I know. And your pizza was very good. I liked it. I also like your guy."

"I don't know that he's my guy," she said. "But I should probably go find him." While she and Kate had been talking, the men had disappeared.

"He's in the game room. They were talking about

setting some video game record. Reid seems to be as competitive as you are."

"This whole group is competitive," she replied.

"He does fit right in," Liz agreed. "Maybe you should keep him."

"Maybe you should mind your own business."

"Well, that's never going to happen," Liz said with a grin.

"I'm going to go see who's winning."

"Can I just say that I think you're the one who's winning?" Liz put in, always happy to get the last word.

She smiled. "You know, I do feel like a winner."

"Then give that man another date," Kate ordered.

"We'll see."

An hour later, after several rounds of video games, Jessica put two sleepy, exhausted kids into the back of Reid's car and then got into the passenger seat as Reid started the engine.

"I'm betting five minutes," she told him, tipping her head toward the backseat.

"Until they're out? I give it three."

She smiled and glanced over her shoulder, already seeing Brandon's eyes beginning to droop. "I might need to change my bet."

"They had a good time."

"The best. Brandon would like to move in with Alex and Andrea, I'm sure."

"A lot of boys would."

"Including you," she teased. "You and Michael were going crazy on that driving game."

"I would have beat him if I'd just gone one more time."

She heard the frustration in his voice. "You really don't like to lose."

"Neither do you," he returned.

"Well, I didn't lose. I won pizza night." She felt ridiculously proud of that accomplishment.

He smiled at her. "Shouldn't it be that *we* won pizza night? I'm pretty sure my chopped onions put the pizza over the top."

"Now you want to steal my thunder?"

"Hey, there's no *I* in team."

"Fine. *We* won."

"I like the sound of that much better." He reached out his hand, and slid his fingers around hers. "Mind if we take the scenic route? It's a clear night."

"Not at all. The boys are already asleep."

As Reid drove down the coastal highway, she had to admit it was a spectacular night, with moonbeams dancing off the dark ocean waters and a myriad of stars twinkling up above. There wasn't much traffic, and at times it felt like they were the only ones on the road.

"This is nice," she said. "Let me know if you want your hand back."

"Not a chance," he said, pulling her hand to his lips to give her knuckles a quick kiss.

The tender gesture touched her. "When is the last time you kissed a woman's hand?"

"I think you're the first, Jess. But then there's not a part of you I don't want to kiss."

"Reid," she protested. "The boys might not be all the way asleep."

"Okay, I'll behave—for now."

His tantalizing promise made her nerves tighten, and her mind immediately jumped ahead with both excitement and worry, but she shoved both emotions away. She just wanted to enjoy the drive.

"I liked your friends, by the way," Reid said. "There are a lot of high achievers in that group."

"They liked you, too."

"So I passed the girlfriend test?"

"You did. I'm sorry they were asking you so many pointed questions—Liz, especially."

"They were all looking out for you. It didn't bother me."

"I think they sometimes feel a little sorry for me."

"Why?"

"Because I did everything out of order: pregnancy, kids, marriage, finishing school, divorce—I haven't exactly followed the same playbook as any of them."

"So you made your own way. That's life. The real question isn't whether they judge you for your decisions—it's if you judge yourself."

She let out a little sigh. "You're a lot more insightful than I expected, Reid."

"It's nice to know I'm beating expectations in some regard," he teased.

"You are." She paused, wondering if she was beating any of his expectations, but she wasn't sure she could ask.

Reid must have read her mind. "Just so you know, you're a lot more competitive and funnier than I thought you would be when I first met you."

"Funnier? I don't recall telling any jokes."

"You have a quick wit. You're good with words. I like that."

She felt the same way about him. They never seemed to have awkward silences. When they were quiet, it felt as good and as natural as when they were talking. There was an easiness about being with Reid. She felt like she could be herself and he wouldn't judge, and that was incredibly freeing. She looked back out at the view, feeling like her life was finally starting to fall into place.

They arrived home a half hour later. Reid marched the sleepy boys upstairs since Joel was going to spend the night on the trundle bed in Brandon's room. She took a moment to let Wiley into the backyard, then went upstairs to help get the kids into their PJs and into bed.

Reid waited at the door as she finished settling the boys in and Wiley took up his place on the foot of Brandon's bed. Then they turned out the light and walked down the stairs together.

It was a strange and wonderful feeling to have Reid by her side, as if he were her husband, Brandon's father, as if they were a family.

She sucked in a breath, knowing she really shouldn't let herself get carried away by that thought. It was far too soon.

When they got to the kitchen, Reid pulled out his phone, a frown on his face as he read a text.

"I hope your sister isn't in jail again," she said.

"No, but apparently the friend she has been staying with has strep throat and the girl's parents think Tara should sleep somewhere else."

"Like your place," she said.

"Yeah, and the girl is also out for winter formal dress shopping, which is very upsetting, because now I'm supposed to help her."

She laughed at the expression on his face. "I'm sure she just wants you to pay, Reid."

"I don't know. She told me the other night that she couldn't believe our mother wasn't going to be around to take her dress shopping. It seemed to be important to her, although I can't imagine why. She buys clothes for herself all the time."

"I think it's more the tradition. It's a special night, and she wants to look pretty. Does she have a boyfriend?"

"There's a kid she seems to hang out with; I don't know if he's her boyfriend, but he's taking her to the formal." He let out a sigh. "I wanted to spend more time with you, Jess."

"Well, I have the boys, so…"

"I didn't mean that. I just wanted to talk to you. I like talking to you."

"I like talking to you," she whispered, as he grabbed her hands. "But you should probably go home and deal with your sister."

"She has a key to my place."

She smiled. "There will be other nights."

"Will there? Does that mean I'm getting my fifth date?"

"I think you are," she said.

He gave her a long, hard kiss, as if he wanted to make sure she didn't forget it, and then he said, "I'll call you tomorrow. Are you going to be around?"

She nodded. "Yes. I want to do something fun with Brandon but we haven't made any plans yet."

"Maybe I could come along."

"I think you have to go dress shopping."

A light came into his eyes. "I just had a great idea."

"I don't think I'm going to like it," she said warily.

"Oh, I think you are," he said, then turned and headed to the door.

"Wait a second. Aren't you going to tell me what it is?"

"Tomorrow," he said with a sly smile.

"I'm going to think about it all night."

"Well, as long as you're thinking about me, I'm good with that."

Fourteen

"I can't believe you're dumping your girlfriend on me," Tara complained as Reid drove them to Jessica's house on Sunday morning.

"I'm not dumping her on you," Reid replied. "We're all going to San Francisco. We'll get you a dress and then we'll ride the cable cars, go down to Fisherman's Wharf and out to Pier 39 to see the sea lions, and have a great meal. It will be fun. You love the city."

Tara gave him a grumpy look. "You could have just said no, Reid, instead of pretending to want to help me."

"I do want to help you. I also want to spend time with Jessica and Brandon." He paused, deciding to be straight with his sister. "Look, Tara, I like Jessica. She's important to me. I want you to get to know her." He glanced at his sister, seeing a softening in her eyes as she gazed back at him. "So can we help each other out?"

"You really like her?"
He nodded. "I do."

"I don't think you've said that about anyone before. Okay. I guess I should get to know her."

"Thanks."

"But you owe me."

"I owe you?" he echoed doubtfully. "I don't think so. The score between us is not even close. Which reminds me, you haven't told Mom about your drunken vandalism the other night, have you?"

"I'd rather tell her when she gets back. She said she's coming home on Wednesday. We'll see if that's with or without a ring on her finger."

"She told me she decided to wait to get married."

"You know how often she changes her mind."

He knew that was true, but hoped that Tara was wrong in this instance. His mother usually made better decisions when she actually took some time to make them.

A moment later, he pulled up in front of Jessica's house. Jessica and Brandon came outside and met up with him and Tara on the sidewalk.

Brandon gave him a happy hug. "Mom says we're going to ride cable cars," he said excitedly.

"We are. And we're going to see the sea lions," he said.

"Do they roar?" Brandon asked.

He laughed. "We'll find out." He smiled over at Jessica. She looked pretty and casual in her jeans and sweater, her hair wavy around her shoulders, dangly earrings hanging from her ears and a pop of pink on her lips. "Hi," he said softly, as a look passed between them.

"Hi," she said, a husky note in her voice.

He cleared his throat, breaking his gaze with Jessica. "I know you met briefly at the firehouse, but this is my sister Tara—Jessica and Brandon."

"It's nice to see you again, Tara," Jessica said.

"Do you want to watch videos with me?" Brandon asked.

While Tara gave Jessica an assessing nod, her smile to Brandon was full of warmth. "Sure. What have you got?"

"I have *Frozen*."

"Cool. I like Elsa."

"You don't have to watch with him," Jessica put in.

"It's fine," Tara said. "You can sit in the front."

As Tara and Brandon got into the backseat, Jessica gave him an uncertain look. "I can't believe this was your great idea."

"It's fine. Tara is totally on board."

"I doubt that."

"It's going to be a fun day. Trust me. I am going to make sure that no one goes home unhappy."

"That's a big promise considering we have an already annoyed teenager and an impatient seven-year-old in the car."

He grinned. "I told you—I like big challenges."

"Then let's go. I'm prepared to be happy."

"And I'm prepared to find a way to kiss you sometime today without those two in the backseat catching us."

"Another big challenge," she said with a laugh, as she got into the car and closed the door.

He walked around to the driver's side and slid in behind the wheel. He might have set some nearly impossible goals for himself, but he had every intention of keeping his promises, especially the one about kissing Jess.

Tara wasn't happy, Jessica thought two hours later as they walked through yet another department store in Union Square. Brandon wasn't happy, either. He kept asking Reid when they were going to get on the cable cars. Reid was trying to be nice to both Tara and Brandon, but he was getting nowhere fast.

"Okay," she said, calling a halt to the rambling meandering that was getting them nowhere. "Here's what we're going to do."

Three pairs of eyes turned to her. "Reid and Brandon, you guys are going to go outside and watch the musicians in the square. Tara and I are going to find the perfect dress. We will meet you in an hour or sooner, depending on what we find."

"Sounds good to me," Reid said with relief in his gaze. "Tara?"

His sister shrugged. "Whatever."

"Good luck," Reid murmured to her, as he took Brandon's hand and headed down the aisle.

She glanced at Tara. "Now that we've gotten rid of your big brother, why don't we try to find a beautiful and sexy dress for your dance?"

Tara's eyes widened, as if surprised by her comment. "Sexy, huh?"

"Of course. It's your prom. Let's go upstairs and find something great without Reid looking over our shoulders."

"All right," Tara said, a little more energy in her voice.

As they went up the escalator, she said, "So who are you going to the dance with?"

"My boyfriend Doug."

"How long have you been going out?"

"Since Christmas, but I'm probably going to break up with him."

"Why?"

"He's going to Chico State, and I'm going to San Diego. We're never going to see each other after graduation."

"I had the exact same problem. My high school boyfriend went to college back east, and I stayed in California. He broke up with me right after graduation. I was sad in the beginning, but when I got to school, it felt good to be free, to not have to worry about him. I could be whoever I wanted to be. I didn't have any strings pulling me back home. I didn't have to be the girl I was in high school, which was very appealing."

"I like that idea. I'm the girl who has a crazy mom who's never around," she said with a sigh.

"Reid mentioned that you've spent a fair amount of time on his couch."

"On a lot of couches," she said with a sigh. "But I'm used to it."

She doubted anyone really got used to that, but she wasn't going to question Tara further. She'd just heard more from Tara in the last fifteen seconds than she had since she'd gotten in the car.

As they got off the escalator, they moved into the dress department, where a dark-blue, mini-dress caught Tara's eye. Without her big brother looming behind her, offering irrelevant suggestions, Tara became a lot more decisive and interested in actually getting a dress.

Jessica tried to help by pulling out possible dresses and holding them up, but never commenting if

Tara didn't like something. She'd just put it away and move on to the next rack.

Eventually, she found herself outside the dressing room while Tara started to try on dresses.

While she was waiting, she got a text from Reid.
How's it going?
Good. Trying on dresses. Brandon okay?
Watching a street magician. He wants to do magic now instead of fight fires.

She laughed at the text, then punched in a response. *He changes his mind every other day.*

Get ready then. There's a guy on stilts here. That might be the next career choice.

She looked up as Tara came out in a tight, dark-red dress. She was somewhat appalled by how much skin she was showing, but she tried not to react.

"What do you think?" Tara asked uncertainly, glancing at herself in a nearby mirror.

She carefully chose her words. "It's very pretty...dramatic."

"Is it too tight?"

"Why don't you try on something else, and then you can compare?" she said tactfully.

"Okay." Tara went back into the dressing room. A few moments later, she appeared in the dark-blue short dress with spaghetti straps. There was no comparison between the two dresses.

"Oh, wow," she murmured. "That's beautiful, Tara."

"I think so, too," Tara said, spinning in front of the mirror. "It's really expensive."

"The good ones usually are."

Tara smiled. "I like it. I want to get it."

She was happy to have a decision so fast. "Let's

do it."

As Tara went to change back into her street clothes, she texted Reid. *Hope you have a high limit on your credit card.*

What's the damage? he asked.

Not sure, but you wanted to make your sister happy, and she's all smiles now.

Then it's worth it.

See you soon.

As she put her phone away, she couldn't help but appreciate the fact that Reid was more concerned with his sister's happiness than how much money he would have to spend on the dress. There was definitely a strong bond between Reid and Tara. While Reid hadn't shown a long-term commitment to a romantic relationship, he was definitely committed to his family, at least until Tara was on her own.

After Tara paid for the dress with Reid's credit card, they moved toward the escalators.

"Thanks," Tara said, giving her a tentative smile.

"I didn't do anything."

"You got rid of Reid."

She smiled at Tara's dry tone. "Well, that wasn't very hard. I don't think dress shopping is his thing."

Tara smiled back at her. "No, but you're his thing."

She flushed a little at her words. "We're just...friends."

"Sure you are," Tara said with a knowing gleam in her eyes. "Look, it's fine. You seem nice, and your kid is funny and smart. Just..." She paused for a moment, her gaze turning serious. "Don't hurt him, okay? He pretends like nothing bothers him, but that's not true."

"I know," she said.

"Good."

After leaving the store, they dropped the shopping bag in Reid's car, then the four of them hopped on a cable car and rode it down to Fisherman's Wharf. Brandon loved the cable car ride, excited as the car made its way up and down the steep hills of San Francisco. She hadn't ridden the cable cars since she was about Brandon's age and found it just as much fun as her kid did.

Over the next three hours, they acted like tourists in the city, taking a boat tour around Alcatraz, watching street performers play music, checking out souvenirs and artwork from sidewalk vendors, counting the sea lions lounging on the floating wooden piers in the bay, and eventually eating clam chowder out of sour dough bread bowls on Pier 39, followed by Brandon's favorite thing to do—riding the carousel.

Despite Tara's protests that she was too old for a merry-go-round, they all managed to snag a carousel horse for a ride. With Tara and Brandon in front of her and Reid, Reid extended his hand, and she took it, giving him a smile. Then he pulled her a little closer and leaned over and stole a quick kiss.

"I told you I was going to find a moment," he whispered.

"It took you long enough," she teased.

He laughed. "You're having fun, aren't you?"

"So much," she said honestly. "It's been a great day. You did exactly what you said you were going to do." She tipped her head toward Brandon and Tara, who were laughing and pretending to race each other. "You made everyone happy."

"You helped. The dress shopping was the trickiest part, but Tara seems happy about what she got."

"She looked beautiful in the dress. And it was fun to shop with her. I don't get to do much girl stuff with a little boy in the house. It was a nice change from digging up worms and reading about dinosaurs."

"Tara used to be a tomboy," he said. "We dug up a fair number of worms, too. But she's grown up now. At least she thinks she is. I just hope she doesn't do anything else that's stupid and reckless."

"She's going to be all right," she told him, seeing an unusual shadow of worry in his eyes. "I'm pretty sure you had a hand in getting her to this point. You should be proud of how she turned out."

"That was all her. She didn't have the best parents in the world."

"No, but she had a great brother."

"I tried to be there for her."

"You succeeded." She squeezed his hand and then let go as the carousel ride came to an end.

As he drove back from San Francisco around eight o'clock on Sunday evening, Reid wished the day hadn't flown by so fast, because his good idea had turned out to be better than even he had expected.

After a rough start to the day, Tara had gotten in a much better mood after finding her perfect dress, and the rest of the time she'd been engaged with all of them, especially Brandon. She'd always been good with little kids, and he thought Tara could probably appreciate the fact that Brandon didn't have a dad around, since she'd grown up the same way.

But Brandon was a lot luckier than Tara or him; he'd gotten Jessica as a mom.

He glanced over at Jessica. She started to smile back, then yawned.

"You're tired," he said.

"All that walking and fresh air."

"That will do it." He glanced in the rearview mirror and saw that Tara was listening to music on her phone, with her earbuds in, and Brandon had already drifted off. "Brandon is asleep."

"He's always fallen asleep quickly in cars. When he was little, I used to put him in the car and drive around the block when he was being cranky. It worked every time." She settled back in her seat. "I wish tomorrow wasn't a school day."

"It's a work day for me, too."

"When will you be off again?"

"Thursday. This week is a seventy-two-hour shift followed by four days off."

"Is it weird to work that many days at a time?"

"I've gotten used to it. The flip side is that I get more days off strung together."

"And that's when you surf?"

"I usually do get some surfing in," he admitted. "But I do other things, too. A retired firefighter is now a paint contractor; I sometimes pick up work with him. I also bartend at Micky's, if they need anyone. I keep busy."

"It sounds like it." She paused, tilting her head to the right. "I don't know where you live. Is it an apartment? A house?"

"I rent an apartment two blocks from the beach. I'll have you over some time, if you give me a sixth date."

"I've lost count of how many dates we've had," she said with a grin.

"I haven't. I think we should keep going out."

She glanced back as if to see if Tara was listening to their conversation, then turned to him. "I'm kind of leaning in that direction myself."

He was shocked. It was the first time Jess had acknowledged that they were in fact starting a relationship. "That's good to hear," he said lightly.

"Just so I don't have to keep track of how many dates we're on."

"I've got that. So we'll see each other again when I'm off work?"

"It will have to be Saturday. Friday night is my mother's birthday, and I'm taking Brandon there for dinner." She hesitated. "I'm sorry that I can't invite you. Things are too rocky with my mom's illness to bring a new person into the mix, and to be honest, I don't like them to get too deeply into my life. They always have so many opinions."

"You don't think they'd like me?"

"I didn't say that."

"Because I've always done well with parents."

"Really?" She gave him a questioning look. "You told me you'd never dated anyone longer than a year, so how many parents have you actually met?"

"A few, and we always got along."

"Well, it wouldn't be your fault if you couldn't get along with my parents. They are very difficult."

"I'd still like to meet them."

"You will—sometime. My mom is finishing up her chemo next week, so after that, hopefully everything will get back to normal."

"I'm glad she's going to be all right."

"Me, too."

He stopped at a light. "I can drop Tara off at my place first and then take you and Brandon home."

"I don't think that's a good idea, Reid. I need to get ready for work tomorrow. It's best if you drop us off first."

"All right. We'll get together next weekend then."

"Next weekend," she agreed. "But it seems like a long time from now."

He felt exactly the same way.

Fifteen

After a week spent working and only talking to Jessica on the phone or by text, Reid was more than ready to see her again on Saturday. Since ideal ocean conditions had made Revolution a go, they'd agreed to meet at the bluff overlooking the beach at noon.

She'd asked him several times if he was going to accept a wild card into the competition, and he hadn't been able to come up with an answer. It was crazy to even consider it, but as he walked along the beach just after eight a.m. and saw the organizers setting up the judges' platform, he felt an old familiar rush of adrenaline.

This had been his life a long time ago, and memories of being young, reckless, and free ran through his head. On the flip side, he'd also been broke, sleeping in cars, drinking beer, and not doing anything of real importance with his life. That had all changed when he'd become a firefighter. He liked the life he had now. So why was he even contemplating going back to the other one, if only for a day?

As he was pondering that question, Noah Halsey,

one of the local younger guys he surfed with, came strolling by and gave him a nod. Noah had long brown hair that he pulled back in a ponytail and several tattoos on his arms and legs. He was exactly the kind of guy Reid had once hung out with.

"It's a go," Noah said, excitement in his face. "You in, old-timer? I heard they're giving you a wild card."

"I'm thirty, Noah, not on Social Security."

The eighteen-year-old kid laughed. "That's old for this sport."

He supposed it was, from Noah's vantage point.

"Maybe I'll see you out there," Noah said, as he jogged down the beach.

Reid turned his attention back to the ocean. The waves were already huge and with the incoming tide expected to hit at ten, the conditions would grow even more wild, dangerous, and challenging. Only the best surfers in the world would even finish a ride, and he hadn't faced waves like this in a very long time.

His phone buzzed, and he wasn't surprised to see Bill's number flash across the screen. "Hello."

"Are you doing it?" Bill asked shortly.

"Still thinking about it. I'm at the beach."

"How does it look?"

"Like it's going to be a fierce contest."

"Are you going to be among the competitors?"

"Not sure yet."

"You never take this long to make a decision, Reid."

That was true. He'd had a history of acting first and thinking later, but lately that had begun to change, and the cautiousness hadn't just come since he'd met Jess, but with age, and with a job that forced him to pull people out of stupid situations they'd recklessly gotten themselves into. He certainly didn't want the Coast Guard to have to pull him out of the ocean.

"When you did this ten years ago, you had nothing to lose," Bill reminded him. "Maybe you should ask yourself if that's still true. Anyway, I'm heading down there. I'll either see you on the bluff or in the ocean. If you decide to give it a shot, good luck, and try not to kill yourself."

"I will." He put his phone back into his pocket as he folded his arms across his chest and watched the waves rolling into shore. He had about five more minutes to make a decision, and it had to be the right one…

Jessica woke up a little after eight on Saturday. It was the first morning she'd had a chance to sleep past six thirty in over a week, and it felt good. Brandon must have slept in, too, since he usually woke her up long before now. He was probably tired from their late night at her parents' house. It had gone better than she'd expected, her mom and dad actually making an effort to talk to Brandon. Some of her parents' friends had also been there, many of whom she hadn't seen in a long time, and the extra people in the house had made things less awkward.

But with her family obligation out of the way, she was looking forward to seeing Reid today. The week had seemed impossibly long, and their brief communications had not been at all satisfying. It just wasn't the same as seeing him in person, watching his smile spread across his sexy mouth, seeing his blue eyes change colors with the intensity of his emotions, holding his hand and feeling his warmth and strength run through her.

She shivered with a desire and need that was both exciting and terrifying. Despite her best efforts to stay as detached and play things as cool as possible, she was in way over her head when it came to Reid. That didn't bode well for the future, but she wasn't going to think that far ahead.

As she thought about their plans for the day, she wondered what Reid had decided to do about the competition. She picked her phone up off the bedside table to see if he'd left her a text, but he hadn't. She could text him, but a part of her didn't want to know, didn't want to worry. She'd find out when she got to the beach if he was competing or spectating. Hopefully, it would be the latter, but she wasn't sure he'd make that choice.

He'd told her more about his short surfing career over the past few days and how surfing had not only been an escape from his dysfunctional family, but also a place for him to fit in. He'd found friends out there on the waves, people who shared his interest, and who didn't care about what kind of life he was living when he wasn't in the ocean. She was a little surprised that he hadn't felt like he fit in as a teen; he was such an outgoing person now and he seemed to fit in everywhere. But maybe he'd grown into his confidence.

Her bedroom door opened, and Brandon peeked in. Seeing she was awake, he ran across the room, jumping into bed with her. Of course, Wiley wasn't far behind.

As Brandon snuggled up next to her and Wiley

deposited wet kisses on her face, she laughed, feeling loved and happy. This was her world, her little family, and it was damned good.

"Can we go see Reid surf now?" Brandon asked.

"First, we have to have breakfast."

"Then can we go? I want to see him surf."

"I don't know if he'll be surfing, but we will go down to the beach and see what's happening."

"Joel told me that the waves are dark green monsters, and sometimes they eat the surfers." His eyes widened with worry. "Do you think they'll eat Reid?"

"No, that's just a story, honey," she said, silently thanking Joel for putting that image in her kid's head. "We should write and illustrate a story about a surfer boy."

"We can call him Reid," Brandon said with excitement.

She was surprised by the suggestion. Brandon usually liked to name the heroes after himself. "We can think about it. What do you want for breakfast?"

"Blueberry pancakes."

"You got it."

Wiley barked in approval, even though she had no intention of feeding him pancakes.

"Do you think Reid will come over today after he's done surfing?" Brandon asked, as she put on a robe and they made their way down to the kitchen. "He could write the story with us."

"I'm not sure what he's doing later, honey."

"I'm going to ask him. If he doesn't want to work on the story, we could play catch. He told me last week that he could show me how to throw a baseball. Joel's dad is going to coach our team, and he said we should be playing catch now to warm up our arms."

"I can play catch with you," she offered.

Brandon gave her a doubtful look. "Do you know how? You weren't very good at soccer."

"Well, I'm better at hitting a ball than kicking one," she said with a laugh. "And I wasn't that bad."

"I bet Reid is really good at baseball."

Reid could certainly do no wrong in Brandon's eyes. "I'm sure he is."

"Do you think he would come to my baseball games?"

"Well, I don't know. If he's not working, he'd probably like to come."

Brandon hopped into the chair by the kitchen island, as she gathered together ingredients. "Joel said he's going to do Boy Scouts and go on camping trips," he added. "Can I do that?"

"We can look into it."

"I want to put up a tent. Do you think Reid knows how to put up a tent?"

She sighed at Brandon's endless round of questions about Reid, although it occurred to her that these kinds of questions used to revolve around his dad. But he hadn't mentioned Kevin since Reid had fixed his doghouse.

It scared her how much Brandon was starting to think about Reid the way he thought about his father, but what could she do? She'd already gone too far to pull back now. So far Reid hadn't disappointed Brandon. She just hoped it would stay that way.

After parking in a shopping center off Highway 1,

Jessica, Brandon, and Wiley walked a half mile to the bluff overlooking the area of the ocean where the Revolution competition was being held. It was a little before noon, and the bluff was packed with people.

She saw several of her students with their parents, as well as some of Brandon's friends and their families. When she finally got close enough to see the ocean, her gut clenched at the size of the massive waves.

A group of surfers were in the water, and one man was making a run at one of those waves. A loudspeaker coming from a platform on the beach below announced the man's name; it wasn't Reid.

Was he out there in that wild sea? It was impossible to tell from here. She wished she had some binoculars.

"Mommy, there's Joel," Brandon said, tugging on her hand.

She turned to see Joel and his dad, Max, approaching them. "Hi Joel, Max."

"Nice to see you, Jessica," Max said. "Is this your first Revolution?"

"It is. I can't imagine being out there on the ocean."

"Me, either. But it's exciting to watch others."

"Is Reid out there, Mommy?" Brandon asked, tugging on her hand.

"I have no idea. We'll have to listen for his name."

"You know someone in the competition?" Max asked.

"I'm not sure if he's competing or not."

"If he is out there, I wish him luck." Max turned to his son. "Joel, we need to get a move on. We have to meet your aunt at Caffe Roman."

"Can I stay with Brandon?" Joel asked. "Please, Dad."

"He's welcome to hang with us," she interjected. "If that's all right with you."

"Are you sure? My wife's sister is in town, so we're having lunch at the café, but Joel will probably be bored. She's getting married, so there will be a lot of wedding talk."

"I know what that's like. I'm happy to watch him. Is it all right if I take him back to my house when we're done here?"

"That would be great. Thanks, Jessica."

"No problem."

As Max left, she gave the boys a stern look. "There are a lot of people here and it's dangerous to get too close to the edge of the cliff. So no running off. Just sit down and watch the surfers."

"Okay," Brandon said, as he and Joel sat down a couple of feet away.

She let out the leash a little so Wiley could sit down next to them. He was always protective of Brandon.

Looking away from the kids, she focused her attention on the water, watching as a surfer got up on his board, only to be tossed about like a toy in the churning water. He went under a huge roll of white water, and it seemed to take forever for him to come back up. She held her breath, really hoping that wasn't Reid.

Pulling out her phone, she texted him: *We're on the bluff. If you're not in the water, come find me.*

She waited a moment to see if she would get a quick text back, but there was no reply. Her stomach churned with worry. *He wasn't her responsibility. He was a grown man; he could take care of himself.* But she really, really, didn't want anything to happen to him.

"Jessica?"

She turned at the sound of her name. It was Reid's friend Bill. He was out of uniform today, wearing jeans and a dark sweater. "Hi, Bill. Is Reid surfing? He told me he had a wild card if he wanted it, but I haven't heard his name called out, and it's impossible to see anyone from here."

"I don't know. I talked to him earlier; he hadn't decided yet. I gave him my opinion, but he wasn't interested in hearing it."

Reid might not have been interested in Bill's opinion, but she was. "What did you say?"

"That he should leave a pro surfing competition to the pros. He was great a long time ago, but it's been ten years since he was at that level. I understand the idea behind the honorary wild card for former finalists, but maybe there should be a time limit on it."

"Why do you think he wants to do it?" she asked, genuinely curious. "Just for the thrill of it? I know Reid is all about living life and pushing the boundaries, but this seems extreme."

"He does like a big challenge, but surfing is more than that for him. He had a rough childhood, and surfing was where he was the happiest. When he was on the water, he didn't have any family problems."

"I've met Tara, and he's told me a little about his mom and sister, not too much about his dad, though. Did you know him?"

"Never met him. Reid has been the man of the family as long as I've known him. He's always felt like he had to take care of his mom and his sister."

"It's a lot to put on a kid," she said, thinking to herself that she didn't want that to happen to Brandon. She never wanted him to feel responsible for her. He was her child. She was meant to take care of him—not the other way around.

"Well, now that Tara is graduating, he can finally move on. He can take the job in Chicago if he wants," Bill said. "Or he can go anywhere else, for that matter. The sky is the limit."

She frowned. "What job in Chicago?"

At her question, Bill gave her a guilty look. "Uh, Reid didn't tell you about that?"

"No. He has a job offer in Chicago?"

"There's an opening at a firehouse there. I think he applied for it. He has a good chance of getting it if he wants it. But his desire to leave might have changed since we last spoke."

Anger, followed by a wave of hurt, ran through her. In all the time they'd spent together, Reid had never mentioned applying for a job in Chicago. She'd made it clear to him that she was concerned about Brandon getting attached to someone who might not stick around, yet he'd failed to mention he might be moving across the country.

And what about all the things he'd said to her about wanting to keep dating her, about acknowledging that they were in fact having a relationship? Why push for more dates if he was on his way out of town?

"I shouldn't have said anything," Bill said. "I keep sticking my foot in my mouth. I'm sure Reid was going to tell you about it. Or it's possible he's not even going to go."

"I'll have to ask him," she said.

"Looks like you're going to have that chance right now," Bill said, tipping his head.

She turned to see Reid approaching. He was in jeans and a long-sleeved T-shirt, and her first feeling was of relief. He wasn't in the water. He wasn't risking his life to ride a wave.

"Jessica," he said, giving her a warm smile, followed by a quick kiss. "I've been looking for you." He nodded to Bill. "How's it going?"

"You decided not to surf, I see," Bill said.

"I did. I'm leaving the competition to the young titans, not the *old-timers*, as someone called me earlier today."

"Good decision," Bill said. "I haven't seen anyone get a clean ride yet."

"There are very tough conditions, but the third heat coming up has some of the best riders in the world. Jackson Hayes will be out there. He's won four competitions this season," Reid added for her benefit.

She didn't really care about the surfing anymore; she was thinking about Chicago.

"Is something wrong?" Reid asked, giving her a questioning look.

"I'm going to take off," Bill said quickly. "Bye, Jessica."

"Bye," she said shortly.

"Jessica?" Reid pressed.

She glanced away from him for a moment, making sure that Brandon and Joel were still seated and out of trouble, which they were.

"I thought you'd be happy I wasn't surfing," Reid said, calling her attention back to him.

"It's not really my business, is it?" she asked,

unable to keep the hurt out of her voice.

He frowned. "Okay, what did I miss?"

"Bill said you applied for a job in Chicago, and that there's a good chance you'll get it."

"Oh."

She saw the truth in his eyes. "So you're leaving?"

"No—I don't know. I haven't gotten accepted. I haven't even interviewed yet. And even if they said yes, I don't know that I would go."

"Why wouldn't you go? If you applied, it sounds like you want the change. Your sister is going to college. Your mom has someone in her life. You're free to do whatever you want to do."

"All that is true, and that was my thinking when I first heard about the job, which was before you and I went out." He paused. "You have to understand that aside from the several months I spent surfing in between high school and college, I've lived in this town. It's great, but it's small. I've always thought I'd move somewhere else eventually."

"It is small," she agreed. "If you want to make a move, you should make it. I just wish you'd mentioned it. I told you that I was concerned that Brandon would get attached to you, and that's already happened. But obviously there's nothing we can do about that now. When you leave, he's going to be upset."

"Like I said, I don't know that I'm leaving."

"Don't you?" she challenged.

"Hey, Reid," Brandon interrupted as he and Joel and Wiley joined them. "Are you surfing?"

"Not today, buddy. The waves are too big for me."

"I want to be a surfer," Brandon said. "It looks cool."

"Me, too," Joel added.

"We'll have to get you both out on boards one day," Reid said. "Your mom, too."

"Can we, Mom?" Brandon asked.

"I'll think about it," she replied.

Brandon gave her a pouty look. "You always say that before you say no."

"Thinking about it means I'll think about it," she said on a sharper note.

"Mom—"

"If you ask me again right now, it will be no," she told Brandon.

"Fine," Brandon said, crossing his arms, a pissed-off expression on his small face.

She felt a little guilty for her harsh tone, but she did have a lot of things to think about— most importantly whether she should spend one more minute with Reid, knowing that he was probably going to be gone by summer.

"So there's a good surfer in this next heat," Reid told Brandon, directing her son's attention back to the sea. "He has the long yellow stripe on his wet suit. You'll see him in a minute. He's one of the best in the world."

While Reid focused Brandon and Joel on the surfers, she drew in a deep breath and let it out. She appreciated that Reid had taken over with Brandon while she was still pulling herself together, but it also hurt to see him with her son, knowing that moments like these were not going to be a long-term thing. He wasn't sure he was leaving, but she thought he probably should go. She didn't want him to stay for her, to give up his dreams. In the end, he'd resent her. She'd already seen that with Kevin. She couldn't do it again.

"There he is," Reid said excitedly. "There's Jackson." He pointed to the ocean. "Do you see him?"

"He's doing it," Brandon said.

The surfer was amazing, she thought, watching the man skillfully weave his way across the enormous wave that threatened to crush him with white water.

"That's a winning ride," Reid said, glancing back at her. "You just saw one of the best surfers in the world."

"It was impressive," she agreed.

As Brandon and Joel sat back on the ground, Reid smiled that smile that always made her heart flip over in her chest. "I know you're angry, Jess. I wasn't intentionally holding back information from you. To tell you the truth, I kind of forgot about it the last few weeks, and I figured we'd discuss it when it was really an issue."

"I admit that the news surprised me, but you should do what you want to do. I understand that you're coming off some very long-term responsibilities to your family, and the life I have to offer and share is filled with similar commitments. I know I'm jumping ahead by saying that, because we're just starting something, but we both know it's true. We can pretend it won't be an issue, but it will be."

"Jess—"

"Let me finish. I would never ask you to stay here for me, because I did that once before—with Kevin." She lowered her voice, so Brandon couldn't hear her. "I asked Kevin to marry me. I never told you that. I never told anyone that. I let people think it was his idea, that he insisted on taking care of me. But it was me. I was afraid to be alone. I didn't think I could do it on my own. And when he finally left, he told me I'd stolen years from his life."

"That's ridiculous," Reid said sharply. "You were in it together. You didn't do anything to him. You made that baby together."

"But I convinced him to stay with me, and that's not what he wanted to do. Right or wrong, it was a disaster and one I don't care to repeat. I want—*need*—to be with someone who really, really wants to be with me and my kid. And I don't think that's you."

She wanted him to say it was him, but his momentary hesitation spoke volumes.

"We need to talk about all of this," he said finally. "We can't do that now."

"We'll just end up in the same place, Reid."

"We don't have to decide everything this second."

"That's what I've been telling myself since I met you. But I'm getting in deeper every day, and so is Brandon. You're all he talks about. Maybe you won't take this job, but that doesn't mean another offer won't come up. My life is here in Half Moon Bay. I moved to be near my parents, to give Brandon a chance to know them. I have a house, a mortgage, a new job, a big dog. I'm not going anywhere, but I understand if you are. We're just not in the same place. It's no one's fault. It just is what it is." Her heart broke with every word. "I don't think we should see each other anymore."

His face tightened. "Jess, come on. We can't do this here."

"There's nothing to do. It's done."

Anger entered his eyes. "This is wrong, and you

know it. You're not just trying to protect Brandon; you're worried about yourself. You can't take a risk even when you have everything to gain."

"I have more to lose," she said flatly.

"Mommy, I'm hungry," Brandon interrupted. "Can we go home?"

"Yes. You and Joel can play there until his dad picks him up."

"Can you come with us, Reid?" Brandon asked. "You could play catch with me and Joel, so we can get ready for baseball."

"Reid can't come," she said quickly, answering for him.

Reid frowned, but he didn't contradict her.

"But I need to learn how to catch," Brandon whined.

"There's time for that," she told him, not wanting Reid to make a promise she couldn't let him keep. "Say good-bye to Reid."

"Bye, Reid," Brandon said, giving him a hug.

The look on Reid's face when Brandon pulled away almost undid her. He had what appeared to be real pain in his eyes. But he didn't say anything, and neither did she.

As she walked back to her car, she kept telling herself she'd done the right thing; she just didn't know why it felt so wrong.

Sixteen

For the next two weeks, Reid kept himself busy with work and playing mediator between his sister and their mother, who had returned from India with her boyfriend and announced she would still be getting married, but she would wait until after Tara's graduation.

Tara was marginally happy about the decision, although still not thrilled about the new guy in the house. But so far that guy seemed to be okay. He appeared to be genuinely interested in their mother, and he had encouraged her to maintain healthy habits, so maybe it would all turn out well.

Thankfully, he hadn't seen any of them in a few days since he'd been on shift. But now, away from family drama, and the work day in a lull, his thoughts drifted back to Jessica, to their abrupt good-bye at the beach.

Actually, she'd never said good-bye. Brandon had. Jessica had just walked away. He understood her reasons for breaking things off. He knew she was trying to protect Brandon and herself; he'd just never been the guy who someone needed to protect against. And it bothered him that she hadn't really given him a chance to talk things out. He'd texted her a few times, left some voicemails, and eventually he'd gotten a text back that was short and to the point. She was done and she wished him well. *Wished him well...* What the hell kind of thing was that to say to him?

Letting out a sigh, he drew Bill's attention from the equipment they were supposed to be checking.

"Okay, what is wrong with you?" Bill asked. "I've never heard so many sighs from someone who wasn't my girlfriend and wanted me to ask her what was wrong."

"Just tired," he muttered.

"It's Jessica, isn't it? I messed things up for you when I told her about the Chicago job. It just slipped out. I didn't mean to blow up your relationship."

"She would have heard about it sooner or later, although later would have been better. You have a big mouth, Carlton."

"Sorry. What happened?"

"She ended things."

"Just like that?"

"She doesn't want Brandon to get more attached to me if I might leave."

"I hate to say it, but that makes sense."

"Does it make sense? I think it's ridiculous to not enjoy the time we could spend together because of some distant possibility that it might end. Anything could end."

"True. But is it really such a distant possibility?" Bill asked. "What are you going to do about the Chicago job? Do you still want it? Do you still want to move?"

He sighed again. "I don't know. I can't stay for Jessica, and she doesn't want me to stay for her. She wants me to do what I want to do, and I don't know what that is anymore."

"You could stay for yourself. It wouldn't make me sad to have you stick around. We've got a good crew here."

"I know that. I love this firehouse."

"You just want more. I get it. But maybe it's not a new job or a new city that you really want. Seems like Jessica might not be the only one afraid to take a risk."

"I have never been called too cautious," he retorted.

"When it comes to love, you haven't exactly jumped in."

"Because I've never been in love."

Bill smiled. "Are you sure about that?"

Before he could reply to that question, the fire bells went off.

Quickly putting the equipment away, they went into work mode, and soon they were on their way to a house fire.

The two-story home was engulfed with flames when they arrived a little after five p.m., the fire a wash of orange against a darkening sky. Their truck was the first on the scene. A neighbor came rushing toward them as they jumped off the truck.

"There's an elderly couple who lives there," a middle-aged woman said. "My husband tried to go in, but there was too much smoke."

Reid could see a man pacing around the perimeter of the house.

"We've got this," his captain told the woman.

"McAllister, Carlton, check out the house."

As he and Bill ran into the house, the other firefighters set up to attack the fire.

"You take the first floor, I'll take the second," he told Bill, pulling down his face mask as he jogged up the stairs. The heat and smoke got thicker as he reached the second floor. Flames leapt out of the ceilings and walls. He wasn't sure where the fire had started, but it was in full force and judging by the color of the smoke, it was getting worse by the second. "Fire department, call out," he yelled, making his way down the hall. He checked the first room; it was empty. Then he heard a whimper.

He ran down the hall and into what was probably the master bedroom to find an elderly man sitting on the bed next to a woman who appeared to be unconscious. There were no flames yet, just thick, black smoke.

"I can't get her up," the man told him, coughing with each breath.

He checked on the woman, who had a pulse, but it was faint. "Can you walk?" he asked the man.

"Yes, but I'm not leaving her. When she goes out, I go out," the man said, getting to his feet. "We've been married for fifty years. If she doesn't make it, I don't want to live without her."

"I have one unconscious female, one male, second floor," he said into his headset. "Coming down now." He turned toward the man. "I'll carry her out. You go first."

The elderly man headed toward the door, but he'd barely gotten there when an explosion rocked the house, blowing out the windows and knocking the man off his feet.

Reid instinctively threw his body over the woman, just as half the ceiling came down on the back of his head and everything went dark.

Jessica grabbed her phone off the kitchen counter, stirring the simmering spaghetti sauce with one hand as she said, "Hello?"

"It's Kate, Jess. How's it going?"

"Good. What's up with you?"

"Just checking in. I'm sorry you missed the bachelorette party."

"Me, too, but I just couldn't make Vegas work," she said. "Did you have fun?"

"A lot. I'm sure you saw some of the photos. I have more I can send you, too."

"I'd like that."

"I still feel bad we couldn't get you there."

"Please do not worry about it." Besides not having a babysitter for a weekend trip, she'd been happy to sit out the bachelorette party in her current, somewhat depressive mood.

"All right. Well, my next question is about seating arrangements at the wedding. Are you bringing your handsome firefighter?"

"Oh. No. It will just be me and Brandon," she said, feeling another wave of sadness at the thought. It had been two weeks since she'd seen Reid, but it felt like two years. She'd told herself the pain would have been even worse if she'd let things go on, but she was having a hard time believing that now.

"Sorry to hear that. Is he busy or…"

"We're not seeing each other anymore."

"Really? But you seemed so happy with him at pizza night."

"He's a great guy, but our relationship has nowhere to go. We're just not in the same place, and I have a lot of baggage."

"I think you're worth the bags you bring with you."

"That's sweet of you to say."

"And it's true."

Kate's sympathy made her heart hurt a little more.

"How are things going with the wedding?" she asked. "Everything still running smoothly?"

"So far. But we have a month to go, so I don't want to jinx it."

"I'm sure it will be great. You do amazing weddings."

"I'm getting a lot of practice. I just want each woman to have something that's special just for her."

"I haven't heard any complaints."

"Thanks. I'll let you go. Let me know if you want to bring someone else to the wedding. See you soon."

"Bye, Kate." As she set down her phone, she stirred the sauce again, then turned on the television, so she wouldn't have to think about her depressingly single state and the man she'd turned her back on.

She flipped through the channels. There wasn't much to watch early on a Sunday night. She settled for the news, so she could check the weather forecast for tomorrow, but the reporter wasn't talking about rain; she was talking about fire.

Her heart sped up. She scanned the scene behind the newsperson for any sign of Reid, but all she could see were smoke and flames and people rushing around a neighborhood of homes.

As the camera zoomed in on the reporter, she finally heard what the woman was saying, and then her breath caught in her chest.

"A firefighter has been injured in the explosion," the reporter said. "Details of his condition will be forthcoming."

It wasn't Reid, she told herself. He might not be working or if he was working, he still might not be there. She couldn't tell where the neighborhood was. Maybe it wasn't in Reid's territory. On the other hand, Half Moon Bay wasn't that big, and there were several fire trucks in view.

She paced around the room, praying that it wasn't him, that he wasn't hurt. But she needed to do more than just walk around in circles. She needed to know who had been injured. But she couldn't rush across town to a fire scene. She was cooking dinner. She had a child to watch. And she wasn't even seeing Reid anymore.

She just had to wait, be patient, think positively.

As she heard Brandon heading toward the kitchen, she turned off the television, not wanting him to worry, too.

"Is dinner ready?" he asked, as he came into the room. "I'm starving."

"It will be in a few minutes," she replied, trying not to show the turmoil inside her.

"Can I watch TV?"

"No," she said harshly.

"But—"

"No," she repeated. "You can read a book or do some drawing until dinner is ready."

He frowned but went to get a book from the family room shelves. Then he settled on the couch and started reading to himself.

For the next hour, she tried to concentrate on cooking, then having dinner with Brandon, but mentally she was only ten percent there. The rest of her brain was on Reid.

This kind of worry was just another reason for her not to be involved with him, she thought. She didn't need extra stress. It was enough to worry about her child every minute of the day.

But even though the argument made sense, all she could think about was how abruptly she'd ended everything. He'd texted her several times, but she'd only answered once and that was to say she wished him well. *What the hell had she been thinking? How could she have been so cold to him?*

What if he wasn't okay? What if the last memory she had was of that awful, cold text?

She didn't want to think that he wasn't going to make it, but she couldn't help herself.

And she mentally kicked herself for wasting the last two weeks. What if she could have spent those days with Reid—had more time with him?

Why had she been so afraid?

This was what real fear was about.

She'd been scared of getting her heart broken when she should have been afraid of losing out on being with an incredible man.

Maybe he would have left her in the end, but at least she would have tried. When had she stopped trying?

Years ago.

She wanted to blame it all on Kevin, but she couldn't. It was her fault, too. Since her divorce, she'd been like a turtle, tucking her head into a hard shell and hiding away so no one could get to her, no one could cause her pain, but she'd missed out on some joy along the way.

"Mommy," Brandon said loudly.

"What?" she asked, realizing she hadn't heard a word he'd said.

"Can I watch TV now?"

"You can watch a movie," she said, getting up to help him find a movie on the family room television. She didn't want him to hear about the fire.

Once she had Brandon on the couch watching one of his favorite movies for the hundredth time, she grabbed her phone and went into the living room. She called Reid, but it went to voicemail.

"Hi, it's me," she said. "I saw the news about a fire. I just wanted to be sure you were okay. Let me know." As she was debating what to do next, her gaze fell on the paperwork she'd brought back from the community emergency response class weeks ago. She walked over and picked up the top sheet. Both Reid and Bill's mobile phone numbers were listed on the paper.

She punched in Bill's number. It rang three times, and she was about to hang up when a male voice came on the line.

"Hello?"

"Bill? This is Jessica."

"You must have seen the news," he said heavily.

Her heart sank. "Was Reid hurt? They didn't say a name."

"He was. I'm at Mercy Hospital."

Her breath caught in her throat. "Is he going to be all right?"

"I don't know yet, but it's Reid—he's tough."

She drew in a shaky breath. "What happened?"

"Ceiling came down on his head while he was rescuing the inhabitants of the house."

"Oh, my God. Was he burned?"

"We'll know more when the doctor comes out."

"Would you mind calling me and letting me know how he is?"

"I thought you two were done."

"I still care about him, Bill. I care a lot."

"Okay. I'll call you back," he said, not sounding overly excited about the promise. She wondered what Reid had told Bill about her. Bill probably didn't like the way she'd treated his friend, but right now that was the least of her worries.

She went back into the family room and sat down with Brandon. She'd made it through ten minutes of the movie when her phone rang.

She walked quickly out of the room to take the call from Bill. "How is he?"

"He's going to be fine, Jessica. He has a mild concussion and some bruised ribs, but nothing too serious. They'll keep him in the hospital tonight. He should be out tomorrow morning."

"That's great," she said with an immense feeling of relief. "Thank you so much for calling me. I've been so worried. I've been going crazy here."

"No problem. I told you he was tough."

Her eyes blurred with tears of relief. "You did."

"Hey, Jess?"

"Yes?"

"Tell Reid how you feel. Sometimes you don't get a second chance. My unsolicited advice."

"Thanks, Bill."

She hung up the phone and felt like doing a little

dance around the living room; she was so happy to know Reid would be all right. She took a couple of deep breaths, then went back into the family room. She tried to concentrate on the movie again, but she still felt restless.

Was anyone with Reid? Had Bill called Tara? Was his mom back in town?

She had a lot of questions and no answers. She couldn't just sit here and do nothing.

After several more minutes of internal debate, she called Hayley to see if she could babysit. Then she told Brandon she would be back in an hour and made her way to the hospital.

Seventeen

As Reid shifted in bed, he winced at the pain shooting across his head.

"You need something for that?" Bill asked, giving him a concerned look.

"I already had something," he replied. "I'm fine."

"Good thing you have such a hard head."

"Yeah," he said, trying to get into a more comfortable position, but everything hurt. "How's the elderly couple? They made it out, right?" He vaguely remembered someone telling him that in the ER, but he wanted to be sure.

"Yes, they're being treated, but word is they will both recover."

"Good." He was relieved to know that they'd gotten out safely. The older man's devotion to his wife had been something to see. "You should go back to the house. Shift isn't over yet."

"I know. I'm going now. Hopefully the rest of the night will be uneventful." Bill walked to the door, then paused. "I spoke to Tara and told her you were all right. She said she'd pass that on to your mom. And

I don't know if you want to hear this, but Jessica called."

His pulse leapt. "She heard about the fire?"

"She saw it on the news and called me. She was really worried about you. I thought you might want to know."

"Thanks."

"I'll see you tomorrow."

As Bill left, his thoughts turned to Jessica. She'd called about him, concerned for his well-being. He supposed that was something, but on the other hand, the fact that he'd been injured while fighting a fire and doing his job had probably given her another reason to stay away from him. Not that she'd needed one. She already had a very long list of reasons.

Closing his eyes, he let out a weary sigh, thinking about the old man who'd refused to leave his wife, even though he could have perished along with her. He'd said they'd been married fifty years. That was amazing. They'd spent so much of life together; they were true partners. He hadn't seen an example of that kind of love in his family. He hadn't even really believed it existed. But now he couldn't seem to stop thinking about it—and about Jessica.

He heard the creak of the door and opened his eyes, a little shocked that the image from his head had just materialized in real life. He blinked, wondering if he'd conjured her up somehow, but as Jessica walked over to the bed, she looked very real. Her dark-brown hair was caught up in a ponytail, her brown eyes were filled with worry, and there were shadows under her eyes, made more pronounced by the paleness of her skin. *Were those shadows just from tonight or from the last two weeks?*

"Hi, Reid," she said softly. "How are you feeling?"

"I'm okay."

"You don't look okay."

"A bump on the head—no big deal. I've been hit worse by my surfboard."

"I heard something about a roof falling on top of you, so I doubt that."

"Bill always exaggerates." He drew in a breath. "It was nice of you to come down here."

"I couldn't seem to stop myself."

"Sounds like you tried."

She met his gaze. "I wasn't sure you'd want to see me."

"I always want to see you," he said.

She licked her lips. "I don't know why you would after the way I ended things."

"You were scared—and not just for Brandon."

"You're right. It was as much about me as it was about him. I wanted to protect both of us."

"I understand that you have a long list of reasons for why you and I don't work: dangerous job, reckless hobbies, lack of commitment, might move away, could break your heart, could break Brandon's heart—have I left anything out?"

"That pretty much sums it up."

"Isn't there anything on the pro side of your list, Jess?"

"Of course there are good things—lots of things," she replied. "You're kind and generous and funny. You're smart and handsome. You're a free spirit, and you've made me feel like myself again, like the woman I used to be, someone who could laugh and break rules and have fun."

"You should have fun. You should be that woman again. I actually like her a lot."

"I like her, too."

He took her hand. "You don't have to pay penance for the rest of your life, Jess. You made some mistakes early on, but you're a great mom, and you deserve to be happy. You deserve to have everything you want."

"I really want to be happy, Reid. I want to be happy with you."

"You do?"

She took a deep breath. "Yes. I didn't just break up with you because I was scared you would hurt Brandon; I was terrified you would hurt me. I broke up with you because I was falling in love with you and I didn't know what to do about it."

The pain in her voice, the blurry moisture in her eyes, made his heart turn over. He'd been caught up in anger the last two weeks, judging her for ending things so fast, for not giving him a chance, but now he could see what kind of turmoil she was in. "That's a terrible reason for breaking up with me. And why didn't you say that before?"

She gave him a watery smile. "Because it seemed stupid to tell someone you've only known a few weeks that you're in love with them, especially when they're probably leaving."

He squeezed her fingers. "What if I told you I was in love with you, too? And that I'm not going anywhere?"

"I'd say you're being nice or the bump on your head is making you say things you don't mean."

"I've never been nice enough to tell someone I loved them."

"Never?"

"No. If we're being honest, I'll admit that commitment and a long-term relationship has never been part of my plan. In a lot of ways, I feel like I've been a dad; I practically raised my sister. And I've had to take care of my mother, too. So when I went out with women, I tried to keep those relationships light and easy."

"I understand. And I really don't want to stop you from having the life that you've dreamed about."

He thought about her words, then said, "Today I ran into a house that was on fire, and upstairs I found two elderly people. They were in their late eighties, I think. The woman fell unconscious from the smoke. Her husband couldn't lift her, and he couldn't leave her. He told me they'd been together for fifty years. He wasn't going out until she did. He was willing to die next to her."

"I hope that didn't happen."

"It didn't. They're going to be all right."

"Thank goodness."

"I haven't been able to stop thinking about that man. My father wouldn't have stayed in the house to protect my mother, me, or my sister."

"But you would stay to protect anyone, Reid. That's who you are."

"You're right, I would." He took a breath, pulling her closer. "I want that kind of love, Jess. I want it with you. I'm not taking the job in Chicago or any other job that would disrupt your life. And I want to be there for Brandon as much as I want to be there for you. I know there's still a lot of scary question marks, but if we try to answer the questions together, maybe it won't be so terrifying."

Her gaze filled with hope and amazement. "I just don't want to hold you back, Reid."

"You're not. I have a new dream now," he said. "And you're it. I don't need to move somewhere else to find what I already have—an amazing life and an incredible woman. Instead of breaking up, I think we should go on our seventh date, and then our eighth and our ninth."

"And then we stop counting."

"And then we stop counting," he echoed with a smile. "How does that sound?"

"Wonderful. But you're going to have to say all this again tomorrow when you're not on painkillers or dazed from a concussion."

He laughed, then groaned at the pain that rocketed through his head. "Deal. I will tell you again tomorrow and the next day and the day after that. But I know exactly what I'm saying and how I'm feeling. I missed you so much the last two weeks, Jess. I don't want to go through any more days without you."

"I feel the same way."

"We're going to make it," he added. "I have a good feeling about us."

"I like the word *us*," she said, giving him a sweet smile.

"You, me, and Brandon," he said, wanting to make sure she understood that.

"Don't forget Wiley. He better not be a deal breaker."

"Not a chance. He brought us together."

"Don't remind me."

He grinned. "Oh, I intend to remind you all the time. Now, isn't it time you kissed me already?"

She leaned in and pressed her lips against his

mouth, her kiss filled with love and tenderness. He cupped the back of her neck and pulled her in again for another kiss, one deeper and more sensual, filled with passion and desire. He couldn't wait to get her alone, really alone, so he could show her all the ways he wanted to love her.

A shrieking beep from a nearby machine broke them apart.

Jessica gave him a breathless, worried look. "What's happening? Are you having a heart attack?"

"Probably. You'd be worth it." He laughed. "But I think it's because I pulled out the plug on the monitor," he said, holding up the end of the cord.

A nurse entered the room. "What happened here?" she asked, giving them both a suspicious look.

"The cord came unplugged," Reid said.

"Uh-huh," she said, plugging it back in. "I think it's time for you to rest."

"Or I could just go home," he suggested. "I feel fine."

"I bet you do," the nurse said with a knowing gleam in her eyes. "But you're staying put until tomorrow."

"She's right," Jessica said, giving him a guilty smile.

"You've got one minute to say good-bye," the nurse told her, as she left the room.

"Make it a good minute," Reid said with a laugh, as the nurse left them alone.

Jessica shook her head. "No way. I want you healthy."

"And I want you."

Her eyes darkened. "You have me, Reid. For as long as you want me."

"That's going to be forever."

"I hope so, but it's so fast."

"It doesn't take long to know when something is right."

"But making something last is harder. We both know that."

"And we both know what it takes. We just have to believe in each other. I can believe in you. Can you believe in me?"

"I can," she said with a nod.

"Good. Now, how about one more kiss?"

"Not a chance. You need to rest so you can get your strength back. You're going to need it for all our upcoming dates."

He liked how relaxed she suddenly was now that they'd put their cards on the table and the worries and doubts were gone. "You, too," he shot back. "I have some big plans for us."

"I can't wait." She gave him a cheeky smile from the doorway. "I'll see you tomorrow."

"And every day after that," he promised.

"And every day after that," she echoed.

Epilogue

Four weeks later...

Her men were waiting for her at the bottom of the stairs. Reid wore a dark-gray suit with a maroon-colored tie, his hair styled, his face cleanly shaven, his appreciative grin as sexy as ever. She didn't think she'd ever get tired of looking at him.

Next to Reid was Brandon, dressed in a black suit with a silver tie to match the ushers at Isabella's wedding. In his hand was the satin pillow he would carry down the aisle to present the rings.

Seeing Brandon and Reid together made her heart swell with happiness. In the last few weeks since Reid had gotten out of the hospital, they'd spent every second that they weren't working together.

Reid had shown her how to bodysurf, and he'd taught Brandon how to throw a baseball. They'd cooked together, watched movies, taken bike rides, and they'd even made up a story together, one she could illustrate with a new sense of purpose, a story she might eventually publish.

She'd introduced Reid to her parents, who had shocked her by actually appearing to like him. They'd made an effort to ask him questions about his life. Reid had even gotten her father to go on a walk with him and Brandon. While they'd been gone, her mother had told her that she thought it was time she had another man in her life, someone who would stand by her, who would love her the way she should be loved. It was the first time in her life she'd ever had such a personal and positive conversation with her mom.

The next weekend, they'd gone to Reid's mother's house. They'd met her boyfriend, and they'd been there to take pictures of Tara and her date before they left for the winter formal. Tara had looked amazing in her dress, and she'd been thrilled to have a little attention for a change.

The rest of the time, they'd just been living life together, and it was a sweet, happy life, one her son was thriving in as well. And when Brandon was asleep or with a babysitter, she and Reid had gotten even closer.

All the worries had vanished. She couldn't imagine Reid not in her life, and she was done worrying about the future. Reid had taught her to enjoy the moment, and every moment was better than the last.

"Mommy, hurry up," Brandon said.

She smiled to herself and started down the stairs. "I wanted to make an entrance."

"And you did," Reid said, as she reached them. "You look beautiful."

She beamed under his regard, knowing that the champagne-colored, short, silky dress fit her like a glove. "It's the dress. Kate and Isabella were very kind to the bridesmaids."

"They definitely were," he said approvingly. "I hope you don't outshine the bride."

"Not a chance. You two look very handsome. Are you guys ready to go?"

"We are. Let's do it," he said.

They got into Reid's car and drove a few miles north to Pacifica, where the wedding was being held in a small church on a hillside overlooking the ocean. Her friends had definitely chosen some scenic locations in which to get married.

"I'm going to find the girls," she said, as she got out of the car.

"Brandon and I will hang out together until it's time for him to do his walk down the aisle," Reid said.

"Can we go over there?" Brandon asked, pointing to a gazebo on the edge of the property.

"Sure, we'll take a look around," Reid said.

"Just don't get dirty," she told her son. "At least not until after the pictures."

"I'll keep an eye on him," Reid promised.

"Thanks," she told Reid, giving him a quick kiss.

"I'm going to expect a little more gratitude later," he teased.

"You've got it."

Knowing she was running late, she left Reid and Brandon to explore while she joined her friends in the dressing room next to the church. As she entered the room, she was almost overwhelmed with the flurry of silk and satin, the scent of perfume and hairspray and the sight of flat irons and makeup trays. She'd chosen to get ready at home since she hadn't wanted to bring Brandon to the church too early, but her friends had obviously been here for a while.

"You made it, Jessica," Isabella said happily, moving away from the full-length mirror.

"Oh, wow," she said. "Your dress is gorgeous, and so are you."

Isabella did a little spin in her white gown, the color setting off her dark hair, eyes, and olive skin perfectly. "I hope Nick likes it."

"How could he not? Plus, he loves you; that's all that matters," she said.

"I think it's time for our toast," Liz said.

"You read my mind," Kate said, as she brought around a tray of champagne glasses. "I have sparkling cider for you and Andrea," she added, as she handed a glass to Liz.

"You're both showing," Jessica said, seeing the cute baby bumps her friends were sporting.

"And my baby is kicking up a storm," Andrea told her, moving next to her. "He might be a soccer player."

"He?" she asked.

"It's a boy," Andrea said with a grin.

"That's wonderful. I can't wait to meet him." She turned to Liz. "What about you?"

"We're having a boy, too," Liz replied. "I was kind of hoping for a girl, but now my boy and Andrea's son will probably be best friends."

"I wonder if we'll all end up having boys," Julie put in. "First Jess, now you two…"

"Are you pregnant, too?" she asked Julie.

"No, no, definitely not," Julie said, quickly putting up her hand. "Just saying…our group is expanding in a very male way."

"Speaking of males," Maggie said, giving Jessica a speculative glance. "Word on the street is that you decided to bring a date to the wedding."

"Yes, I brought Reid, and, yes, we're still going out, and things are really, really good."

Maggie squealed. "Yay! I'm so happy, even though I haven't had a chance to meet this wonderful guy yet, but everyone who has met him seems to love him."

"Do you love him, Jess?" Kate asked. "Should I clear my schedule? And, more importantly, am I going to be the last single woman standing?"

"No proposals yet, but he's the one. I've never been more sure," she replied.

There were more squeals of delight, followed up by hugs.

"This is Isabella's day," she protested. "Enough about me."

"Jessica is right," Kate said. "We'll talk about her love life later. Right now, let's take our fun, candid photo before the more formal ones."

They gathered around Isabella and took a selfie and then grabbed their bouquets and headed to the church.

Brandon and Reid were in the vestibule with Michael and Matt. As the guys went to sit down together, she made sure Brandon's tie was straight and the rings wouldn't fall off the pillow. Then she watched him and the flower girl make their way down the aisle before getting in line with her friends.

It was a small wedding, only about fifty people in the church, which was what Isabella had wanted, and as Jessica stood up next to her friends and watched Isabella and Nick share very personal vows to each other, she was touched by the love she could see between them. By the time they kissed and headed back down the aisle, she was wiping her eyes and trying not to smear her makeup.

After the ceremony, they took pictures for a while and then the group dispersed to go to the reception, which was a few miles away. She found Reid and Brandon behind the church near a small pond. Brandon was entertaining himself by throwing pebbles into the pond.

"Are you done?" Reid asked her.

"All done. We can go to the reception now. If we can rein Brandon in," she added, watching her son spin around in the sunshine.

"Our boy does have a lot of energy," Reid said, putting his arm around her. "And he seems to like to make himself dizzy."

"I know. He's crazy. By the way, I like when you call him that—*our boy*," she said, looking up at him.

"One of these days we're going to make it official, Jess. Maybe after our fifteenth or sixteenth date."

She shook her head. "I told you to stop counting. We're together. That's all that matters."

"We are together, and I've never been happier—in case you haven't noticed."

"I feel the same way, Reid. Every day, I fall in love with you a little bit more. I don't know why I was scared of feeling this way, because it's incredible."

"Kind of like surfing the wildest wave."

"Well, I wouldn't know, but if this is what surfing feels like, I might need to take a few more lessons from you."

"Any time," he promised. "But in all seriousness—"

"We're being serious?" she teased.

"Yes. I want you to know that I do want to marry

you. And I want to be Brandon's stepfather. I won't try to take the place of his dad, but I want to be there for him, and I want us to be a family. I want it all."

"Now who's thinking three steps ahead?" she asked, breathless at his words, the intense look in his eyes, the promise of forever.

"I couldn't see the future before I met you. Now it's all I can think about. You told me to go after my dreams, so that's what I'm going to do."

"And here I am—just living in the moment," she said with a laugh. "The tables have turned."

"They sure have," he said with a grin. "By the way, that wasn't a proposal. I'm going to do it up right one day soon."

"Oh, yeah, how?"

"It's going to be a surprise."

"Well, if it's going to be a surprise, don't tell Brandon; he cannot keep a secret."

"Trust me, you'll be the first to know, and it's going to be magnificent."

She laughed. "With you, I wouldn't expect anything else." She wrapped her arms around his neck and gave him a long, loving kiss that made every nerve in her body tingle with happiness and joy. "I feel alive in a way I haven't felt in a very long time," she told him. "That's because of you."

"Actually, I think it's because of Wiley," he joked.

She laughed at the reminder of how they'd met when she was stuck in the doghouse. "You're right. I'll have to give Wiley an extra treat tonight."

"How about giving me an extra treat tonight?" he teased.

"Absolutely," she said. "I have a lot of treats in

store for you."

He groaned. "How long is this reception going to be?"

"Long. But don't worry. It will be worth the wait."

"You're killing me."

"Only with love," she said. "Our forever starts tonight."

"Or right now," he suggested, as he wrapped his arms around her and gave her another head-spinning, breath-stealing kiss.

THE END

About The Author

Barbara Freethy is a #1 New York Times Bestselling Author of 62 novels ranging from contemporary romance to romantic suspense and women's fiction. Traditionally published for many years, Barbara opened her own publishing company in 2011 and has since sold over 7 million books! Twenty of her titles have appeared on the New York Times and USA Today Bestseller Lists.

Known for her emotional and compelling stories of love, family, mystery and romance, Barbara enjoys writing about ordinary people caught up in extraordinary adventures. Barbara's books have won numerous awards. She is a six-time finalist for the RITA for best contemporary romance from Romance Writers of America and a two-time winner for DANIEL'S GIFT and THE WAY BACK HOME.

Barbara has lived all over the state of California and currently resides in Northern California where she draws much of her inspiration from the beautiful bay area.

For a complete listing of books, as well as excerpts and contests, and to connect with Barbara:

Visit Barbara's Website:
www.barbarafreethy.com

Join Barbara on Facebook:
www.facebook.com/barbarafreethybooks

Follow Barbara on Twitter:
www.twitter.com/barbarafreethy

FIC FREETHY

Freethy, Barbara
Forever starts tonight
: bachelors &

04/16/18

Made in the USA
Columbia, SC
31 March 2018